Oakwood Island – The Awakening

ISBN: 978-1-951122-03-4 (Paperback)
ISBN: 978-1-951122-04-1 (ebook)
LCCN: 2019948874
Copyright © 2020 by Angella Cormier and Pierre C Arseneault
Cover Design: Angella Cormier
Cover Photos: Angella Cormier (front photo) and Pierre C. Arseneault
(back photo)

Printed in the United States of America.

Shadow Dragon Press
9 Mockingbird Hill Rd
Tijeras, New Mexico 87059
www.shadowdragonpress.com
info@shadowdragonpress.com

Visit the author's websites:
Mysterious Ink - www.mysteriousink.ca
PCA Toons - www.pcatoons.com

You can also follow Mysterious Ink on Facebook at:
Facebook: Mysterious Ink - Pierre C Arseneault & Angella Cormier

Twitter: @AngellaCormier / @PierreCArsent
Email: Angella@MysteriousInk.ca / Pierre@MysteriousInk.ca

Other titles by
Angella Cormier and Pierre C Arseneault

Oakwood Island

2016 Best Book Awards: Award-Winning Finalist in the Fiction:
Horror category
2016 Paranormal Book Awards Semi-Finalist
2016 Foreword INDIES Finalist (Horror: Adult Fiction)
2017 New Mexico/Arizona Book awards Finalist - Fiction (Other)

"If you're a fan of good old-fashioned death, blood and gore, like Stephen King books and mystery - this is a must read!" Sarah Butland, author of *Blood Day*.

Dark Tales for Dark Nights

Titles by Pierre C Arseneault

Sleepless Nights
Poplar Falls: The Death of Charlie Baker

Titles by Angella Cormier

A Maiden's Perception: A Collection of Thoughts, Reflections and Poetry

OAKWOOD ISLAND
THE AWAKENING

Written by :

Angella Cormier
and
Pierre C. Arseneault

Shadow Dragon Press
Albuquerque, New Mexico

Table of Contents

We dedicate this book to our families, our friends and our readers. We appreciate your continued support with our stories.

We also want to dedicate this book to all the people who make small towns thrive: To the lighthouse keepers, firefighters, police officers, paramedics, ferry operators, waitresses and waiters, nurses, doctors, store clerks and all the people who make life in small communities the gem that they are. To you, we say thank you. You have been the inspiration for many characters of Oakwood Island that we love to write about and we hope you enjoy reading about too.

A sincere thank you to our publisher and editor, Geoff. Thanks for all your guidance with edits for this book and your dedication to the writing community.

Prologue
Year: 1898

Bessie Chapman was kneeling in the middle of the corn field among the wilting crops. She was patiently listening to the voice speaking to her, staring intently in the direction of the voice even though nobody stood where the voice came from. It sounded as though the wind itself was talking. She had been listening every night for a week. Tonight, she would do the bidding the voice asked of her.

"But how will I know what to carve on this blade?" she asked the voice.

"I will guide your hands. I will carve the symbols with you. But first you must prepare the soil. The earth, fire, wind and water must all be prepared, as does the spirit of the child."

Bessie looked down at the lone rib bone she had taken from the grave where her grandfather was buried.

"Do you promise to provide as you say you will? How can I know for certain?"

"You must not question my commands!" The voice became loud and angry. "You must put all of your belief and intention; else this will not come to be!"

"I understand. I will! I promise! Just please, spare me and my children." Bessie pleaded.

"Now, go to the clearing. Place five points upon the ground, and recite the words I will whisper. You must make haste. Time is fading. Soon, the birth will be upon us. You must prepare the soil with the bone. Next we will carve the symbols. I will guide you."

"How will I know when the child will be born?" Bessie asked.

"Trust my guidance."

Bessie stood up, taking the rib bone in one hand and a chisel in the other. She ran in the dark towards the clearing, eager to do as she had been guided by the voice.

She never noticed the hundreds of crows sitting in the dying corn field, watching her run.

Chapter 1
An Eerie Discovery
May

"**D**o you think it was a werewolf, like that kid always said it was?" Tracy asked her husband as she carried an armload of cut wood to their small utility trailer. The other stacks of wood in the trailer rattled as she dropped in the new load. She pulled up the zipper on the spring work coat she wore, the air still holding a chill as the last bit of snow melted away in the forest. Across the clearing, Michael swung his axe down hard on a log, splitting it in half with a loud crack. The clearing was starting to come together. They'd inherited the house from Michael's uncle, Robert Stuart, and after a lot of work over the past three days the clearing was finally looking less like a wild forest and more like a respectable yard. This project was their latest effort to make a series of connecting trails behind their new home. It was one way to keep Tracy from going completely crazy.

"Trace, I know you want to believe everything you see and read online, but I thought someone like you would perhaps be a *bit* skeptical about monsters and werewolves. I mean, come on. Don't you think maybe you're obsessing about this just a bit too much, hun?" He picked up the two pieces of wood from the loamy forest floor before turning towards Tracy. "I mean, I know you want answers. Hell, don't you think I want some too? Uncle Bob was my favorite uncle. His murder is something I'll never be able to just forget. But I don't want to pretend it was some kind of supernatural monster when the obvious answer is that it was some psycho that took him and Aunt Nancy."

"I know, but there are just too many things that don't add up, Mike. Whoever, or whatever, killed them escaped by the window. Why would a person do that? And by the way," she glared at him with her hands on her hips. "Just because you *think* you know everything, doesn't mean you *actually* know everything."

Mike picked up another piece of wood from the dwindling pile to his right and placed it on the chopping block.

"Good enough, but at least I'm not wasting my time with crazy talk while the case isn't solved." He regretted it as soon as he said it. He looked up to see her already walking away. "Hun, come on. You know what I mean." She was shaking her head no as she walked away from the small clearing.

Tracy hadn't been sold on the idea of leaving the mainland and her career as a legal assistant at Monroe Law Offices. She was now six months into her year-long sabbatical and still didn't know if she wanted to stay on Oakwood Island or return to her job in the fall. Luckily for Michael, he was able to work from anywhere as a stock analyst, so he didn't have to sacrifice his career when they inherited his uncle Robert's house on the island when his aunt and uncle were murdered five years earlier. It had taken four years of vacationing at the home on the island, just to convince Tracy to at least give living here a try. It was a great spot, away from the hustle and bustle from the mainland, and he had always craved returning to the simple life. Convincing his wife Tracy to live here full time, though, had been difficult. He ran to catch up with her on the trail they had created that led to their new home.

"I'm sorry, Tracy. I know what you mean, and I'm sorry.

I didn't want to upset you." He reached out to touch her arm with his left hand. She stopped walking and turned to face him. Tears streamed down her face.

"I know, Mike. I'm just so scared. I wish I could get it out of my head, but I keep thinking about how they were found, their bodies mutilated and ripped apart. We sleep in the same room where this happened! What person could do that? Here, of all places, too!" She took off her oversized work gloves and wiped at her tears. Her emotions were taking over and he knew he had to help her. He had never seen her struggle so much, and he knew he was partially responsible.

"I know, babe. It's not something we can just ignore. But we need to keep our heads clear and focus on what we know as facts. The police and Detective Burke that handled their case did everything they could to find answers. Even now, five years later, the case is still open. Maybe one day we will get answers. Until then, though, we need to live our lives, hun. I want us to really try our best here, even if it gets hard at times." He wiped the rest of the moisture away from the dark circles that had grown larger under her eyes since their move here.

"Can we just take a break? Please?" She let out a deep and slow breath as she finished speaking. Michael nodded in agreement and took her hand to lead her into the woods, off the trail.

"Come on. Let's go for a walk." He pulled her lean body closer to his side, wrapping his free arm around her waist. "Let's go see if there is a spot we can build that meditation hut you were talking about." He smiled at her and she tried to smile back as best she could.

"Fine. But don't think I don't believe in monsters, 'cause I still do. Jerk." She elbowed him in the ribs, chuckling a bit, trying her best to lighten her mood. They walked in a straight line, mostly, for about twenty steps, before both stopped at the same time.

"Mike, do you see what I see?" her voice came out in a barely audible whisper. He nodded and took a few steps closer to the pile of bones that were stacked as high as their knees. She grabbed Mike's plaid work jacket by the left sleeve, forcing him to stop moving. "Don't touch it, Mike. You don't know what those are, or whose. We shouldn't touch anything." Her voice trailed off as he turned to face her, looked in her eyes and took her hand to reassure her. "It's okay, Trace. I won't touch it. I just want to take a closer look, is all. Go to the four-wheeler and get my cell phone. We need to call animal control or something. Most of these are small animals, maybe a deer or two. I'm not sure why they're all piled up like this though."

"Don't you get it, Mike? Don't you see? Whatever killed your aunt and uncle is what did this!" Her tears came back as her voice rose into a panicked cry. "This is why I don't want to be here anymore!" She cried harder as she turned around and ran towards the main trail they had cleared in the woods.

"Just get the phone, Trace. Everything will be okay."

He felt horrible. He knew he had pushed her into coming to live on the island. He knew she was unhappy here yet he wanted to live on the island. As she ran to get the phone he turned back to the pile of animal carcasses and focused on the one that had caught his attention, and the reason why he had sent her away from the scene. Moving in closer he knew for sure now what he was looking at. The femur that protruded from the bottom of the pile was clearly human. Knowing he couldn't let her see this, Mike turned from the stack of bones and ran after Tracy.

Animal control arrived within an hour, and the police shortly after. A lone crow circled the area above the Stuart's house and its new occupants. The island shuddered in the cool wind as a new wave of darkness cast over the skies above.

Chapter 2
Fifth Anniversary
June

The ranch-style house that sat at the end of Montague Lane on Oakwood Island was as typical a house as one could expect, yet its quaint appearance welcomed its owners and visitors with warmth and a sense of welcome that was not typical for the neighborhood. The wrap around ground-level porch gave a feeling of protection. The pillars that stood every six feet gave the illusion of strong arms holding up the top half of the home. The soft yellow siding and olive tone on the shutters created a mellowing effect that nobody could deny was calming as soon as it was seen. Coupled with the curbside appeal of freshly cut lawn, the well-maintained shrubs and the overflowing flowerbeds gave the property the fresh and clean look that most searched for in a neighborhood.

It was a sharp contrast to the cement and paved yard where Scott Cudmore had grown up. The Open Arms Orphanage had always felt bleak, oppressive and even depressing in its appearance to both the kids and visitors alike. Having grown up in such a disparaging environment, he was proud to be a homeowner now and took the time necessary to maintain the property. His pride was apparent to anyone who visited their street. On this particular Saturday morning, he had taken care of cutting the lawn and cleaning the driveway of debris and dirt. With his outside chores completed, he contemplated his plans for the rest of the day. He knew he would eventually need to take care of entertaining the kids somehow, but for now, he decided he wanted a bit more alone time. It was a rarity that he embraced when he could.

In a nook off the side of the kitchen, Scott sat at his roll-top desk enjoying a rare moment of quiet with a cup of dark roast coffee. Few and far between were the moments he could take in some reading time in this modest house, which had been renovated to have six bedrooms instead of the original four. The usual hustle and bustle of having a family was one thing, but to have eight foster kids between the ages of four and seventeen under one roof was often plain chaos. Saturdays, however, were much easier as the older kids could help out with taking care of the younger kids while he worked on whatever weekend chores he had planned. Though it was still work, he felt relieved to have some reprieve from the round the clock parenting role he had so willingly signed up for years prior. He had always questioned if he had what it took to be a good dad. He often imagined how different his life might have been if he had chosen to leave Oakwood behind and start over, somewhere new and without foster kids. He felt a tug in his heart, knowing he never could have chosen a different life. He could never have done so while knowing how those kids felt on a daily basis, as he too had felt the loneliness and sadness so often while growing up at the orphanage.

Scott sat back in his faded leather chair, his hand wrapped around his warm mug with #1 DAD written in big bright letters across the front. He continued reading the most recent issue of The Oakwood Chronicler. The biweekly newspaper normally featured the minor on-go-ings of small town life on the island. Although Scott didn't normally have time to read the paper, he had wanted to read through this issue as they had published an article about the anniversary of the mysterious deaths that had taken place on Oakwood Island. The anniversary alone would have been reason enough to do a spotlight article, but the recent findings on the Stuart property had created a renewed interest in the topic that had set the small population abuzz with gossip.

The recent discovery had prompted the paper to write a piece as this was reminiscent of the strange events that had plagued the island's residents, five years prior. Scott brought his mug to his lips, sipped the warm coffee and read the front page article.

OAKWOOD ISLAND MURDERS –
FIVE YEARS LATER
BY: NICOLE BANFORD

Oakwood Island residents continue to seek answers nearly five years after multiple gruesome murders remain unsolved. Islanders are demanding answers and pressing the issue to the mayor and town council after a report was made about the newly discovered cluster of animal carcasses that was found last month. The animal remains were found on Michael Stuart's property on Ocean's Edge Road. Islanders will remember that Michael's aunt and uncle were found murdered in their home five years ago. Michael and his wife, Tracy Stuart, made the discovery in the woods behind the home. "The snow and ice likely kept them from decomposing completely," Michael told the Oakwood Chronicler in a phone interview. "We just happened to come across the pile. I don't know how long it was there for, but it had to be at least close to a year."

Mr. Stuart contacted the police immediately fol-

lowing this discovery, knowing it was likely important to the unsolved cases that still plague the island
and its residents to this day. The police declined any
further comment regarding the remains, stating that
the discovery was a collection of dead animals, likely
dragged to the area by natural scavengers. When
asked if there was a connection between the remains
and the ongoing investigation of several open cases,
the police advised that no, it did not have any connection. When pressed further with the information
that Michael Stuart had claimed to have clearly seen
a human femur in the pile, the police representatives
questioned Mr. Stuart's ability to tell the difference
between animal and human bones. Then they declined
any further comment regarding the discovery.

The dead animals were only one piece of a much
larger mystery on Oakwood Island five years ago.
Several cases, most still unsolved, placed Oakwood
Island on the map.

Strange occurrences began on the island as much
as a year prior to the first murder. On top of the clus-
ters of dead animals, around the same time some witnesses claimed to have seen what they described as
a werewolf-like creature. It was seen attacking animals and prowling in some backyards of island residents. Although the creature was likely a large bear or
another natural predator, nothing was ever concluded
as to what this creature may have been. If that was
not enough to keep the police department occupied,
there was also the case of Maggie Foster, the victim
of an alleged abduction and who was stricken with a
strange illness. Ms. Foster's symptoms were unlike
anything seen before at the Oakwood Island Hospital,
and her doctors were, and still are, baffled as to what

illness she had and where she contracted it.

The murder cases include those of Robert and Nancy Stuart, whose bodies were found in the bedroom of their home. Only days before, they had found themselves trapped in their car and someone had tried to break in to harm them. It was never known who attacked their car. Their bodies were found, victims of a brutal murder only a few days later.

The Watson family murder is another case that remains unsolved. The bodies of Lawrence, Kathleen and their son Eddie Watson, were all found in their home, their deaths similar to the Stuarts, brutally disfigured and dismembered.

(Continued on page 3)…

Scott's mug thumped against the wood of the desk as he put it down a bit too hard. He brought his hands to his head, massaging his temples as he could feel a slight pressure begin to form around his forehead, tightening its grip with each new line he read. It upset him to read about the anniversary of the killings, but he felt he needed to finish the article, it was the least he could do after so many lives were lost and affected. He turned to page three of the newspaper and scanned the page until he found the rest of the article.

The death of Officer Ryan McGregor is still an unsolved case as while the accounts and evidence for his murder match the mutilations of the Stuarts and the Watsons, who killed them all remains a highly debated mystery. While claims of a wolf-like creature that walked upright are being dismissed by authorities, witnesses such as Oakwood Island's own Jack

Whitefeather insist otherwise. Jack claims in his own words that he saw Ryan being attacked by a monster, a werewolf of some sort.

We spoke with Dr. Monique Richardson, the head of psychiatry at the Daye Psychiatry Unit at Oakwood Island Hospital to get some clarity around the sightings that many believe were a werewolf.

"It is my professional opinion that Jack could not tell the difference between what he believed he was seeing and what really happened to Officer Ryan McGregor. This is something that is very common as hallucinations appear very real, are real, in fact, to the person experiencing them. I believe he wanted to see a werewolf and so is convinced he did." When asked about the other reports by local residents of a monster or werewolf sightings on the island, the doctor confirmed that as with all tragedies, people try to find a common ground and will formulate their ideas of what their senses are experiencing to correlate with those of others, such as has been reported in cases of mass mania. The doctor expressed her disdain in regard to the notion that Maggie may have been the monster many claimed to have seen. Most residents believe there was a serial killer in their midst, who has long since moved on to the Mainland.

However, others believe Maggie's guilt is what drove her to commit suicide at the hospital and that she had been the one responsible for the terror that was brought upon the island five years ago.

"Maggie was a patient at the hospital, a victim herself of a horrible abduction and attack," Dr. Richardson said. "Most of these events occurred while she was being treated and battling for her life. Monsters are not real, people are. A person is responsible for all these horrible things, but it wasn't Maggie. That is my professional opinion."

During the months and years following all these strange occurrences, the residents of Oakwood Island banded together as a community to help each other heal from the senseless killings that changed their lives forever. Some residents claimed this once quiet piece of land would never be the same again, while others continued living their lives with the hope that the answers they seek will one day bring peace and understanding to their community. Five years later, this still holds true.

Scott's eyes scanned over the article again to re-read the sentence about how some of the residents of Oakwood Island had speculated that one of his closest friends, a fellow ward of the Open Arms Orphanage, had been a monster, a supposed werewolf, capable of murder. While he knew that was total nonsense and that he shouldn't let that bother him, Scott couldn't help but feel hurt. His best childhood friend, who always felt more like a sister to him, didn't deserve to have her memory tainted in such a way. Scott downed the rest of his lukewarm coffee in two large gulps before he folded the newspaper in a hurry and shoved it into the trash can that sat under the desk.

Closing his eyes, he recalled Maggie's smile and how it had never faded throughout their childhood. No matter how difficult their lives had been through the years, she always smiled through it all and made sure to make him smile often too. He paused and listened to the abnormal quiet of a Saturday morning. The ticking of the large grandfather clock that stood in the hallway resonated in short, rhythmic pulses. He rarely heard the soft ticking sound of this favorite time piece, a wedding gift from his father-in-law. Today he could fully immerse himself in the peaceful sound that helped to calm his troubled mind after reading the article, but especially some of the vicious messages some people had written on social media about his long-time friend. As he took in a few deep breaths, he could also hear some birds chirping outside, from the opened window that faced the front of the house. The only thing that would make this moment better, he thought, was if his wife, Miriam, was sitting here with him, enjoying the tranquility, instead of working the morning shift at the Oakwood Island hospital, where she was a nurse.

Samantha Myers, the eldest of the foster kids at seventeen, was outside watching the three youngest of the family as they played in the backyard. Lily and Patrick Jones, who were four, and Gavin Williams, aged six. Bradley Shaw, who had recently turned fifteen, was alone in his room, as usual. The other three young boys, who were also known as the Davis brothers were Clay, eight, Peter, ten, and Colin, eleven. The trio were playing video games while wearing the headsets his wife had bought them the previous Christmas. Heavenly quiet was rare in this house full of foster kids, although more often than most, Scott preferred the racket of the kids being kids. This appreciation for the sound of children was no doubt developed during his years of growing up in a busy orphanage, where he got used to the semi-constant buzz of activity and conversation. But occasionally, peace and quiet was nice.

Opening his eyes, he reached for his computer mouse and refreshed his computer. He made his way onto the Facebook page of Oakwood Island's only surviving newspaper with the intention of letting them know exactly how he felt about the article in today's paper. As suspected, the page already had a long thread discussion about today's article. He skimmed the good and bad comments in search of the ones specifically discussing his late friend Maggie.

Scott, much calmer and determined to set the record straight, began typing. He would remind the oblivious fellow residents of the scarred island that Maggie had not had an easy childhood. Having been raised together in the Open Arms Orphanage, Scott had been the closest thing to a brother Maggie had known. He would not sit by while people marred her name with such nonsense. He wanted to honor her memory, and so he would tell them about the good person Maggie Foster had been.

Six-year-old Gavin had dug a large hole in the sand on his side of the shaded sandbox. He was sitting next to it while playing with a toy dump truck and toy loader. An average sized boy, he had thick dark hair, big brown eyes and olive-toned skin. He loved playing in the sandbox and would come out to play in it every day when the sun was out.

Four-year-old twins Lily and Patrick sat back to back on the other side of the large sandbox. Both of them were small for their age, both in height and weight, as was normal for multiples. Their physical traits were very similar. Both had hair that was a butterscotch brown color, bordering toward blonde in shade. Their skin was a very light tone, pale even, and both were speckled with freckles on cheeks and across their nose. Lily had three naked Barbie dolls in front of her. She got onto her knees, her bright yellow and pink sun dress pooling around her as she began digging a small hole in the sand with a red plastic shovel. Patrick wearing his large sunglasses, a blue pair of shorts and grey t-shirt, sat directly behind his sister where he could feel her presence. He patted the ground until he found what he was looking for. He had a stack of blocks between his spread legs and had been missing one; the one with the letter E and the raised picture of the elephant. The block also had a side with a Braille version of the letter E as well. He felt the stack and found the one he wanted. He spoke the letters softly as he felt the blocks one by one.

"There's the E, like E for Elephant." His voice was almost a whisper, he spoke so low. Neither Lily nor Gavin paid any attention to him, each of them carrying on with their own preferred toys.

Samantha sat under the large oak tree in the back yard, chewing on her favorite necklace, as she often did when she read. The sky was blue, not a cloud in sight and the sun was the warmest it had been all season. A slight breeze every once in a while would ruffle her black hair. It was long and straight and she often wore it pulled back into a tight ponytail, her bangs falling just below her eyebrows. She had bright blue eyes that contrasted well against her long and full lashes. She was the type of teenager that was stunning but yet didn't recognize her own beauty. She sat facing the kids, her nose buried in a book as usual, today's selection being the second to last in the Harry Potter series. Samantha was hooked after the initial pages of the first book in the series. Something about the magic element fascinated her. She often would spend entire days lost in a book, where her imagination was free to travel to new worlds and meet incredible characters. It was her preferred form of escapism ever since she was taken into foster care as a toddler.

Gavin mimicked the sound a loader might make as he scooped sand into the bucket and proceeded to dump it into the box of the toy truck. Samantha, the pendant of her necklace in her mouth, glanced over at the children as she turned a page and went back to her book.

"More sand for the new road, Mr. Truck Driver?" Gavin exclaimed as he played. "Sure, LOTS MORE please, Mr. Loader Guy."

Gavin made the sound of the loader again as he prepared to scoop more sand into the bucket. Content with the full load, ready to get dumped in the truck, he started the imaginary conversation between the two drivers.

"That will never be enough sand! Fill it some mo..." Gavin's loud and content play-talk stopped as something caught the six-year-old's attention as he scooped the sand with the tiny plastic loader. A long, slimy worm, striped in shades of black and grey fell from the side of the freshly made hole and wriggled around, sand sticking to its gooey body as it tried to slither in the dry sand. Gavin's palms began to sweat and his throat went dry. Gavin loved crickets, spiders and other crunchy or hairy bugs, but hated slimy, wriggly things like worms. They were gross and he hated everything about them. Gavin swallowed hard as he dumped the sand from his loader, covering the wriggling worm in the process. He scooped up more sand and confidently dumped it over the worm's location, covering it more. Before he could scoop more sand, the worm broke through and wriggled free. Gavin froze as he watched a few more worms wriggling out, these a bit longer and wider than the first one. With his heart pounding and his breathing shallow, he reached for the toy truck with the intention of dumping all its sand over the worms. As his hand reached the truck, he saw more worms had also poked out of the sand in the box of the toy truck. He froze. His mouth as dry as the sand in the play area, he looked at Samantha, hoping she would be looking in his direction, but she wasn't looking. When he turned his attention to the sandbox once more, hundreds of slimy worms were breaking the surface of the sandbox, crawling over top of each other, intertwining their elongated bodies into one large mass of slimy movement. Panic welled up in the six-year-old boy as he struggled to his feet. As he did so, he no longer saw any sand where just mere moments ago he was seated. Worms covered every inch of the sandbox, a large and ever growing puddle of wiggling worms, until they began spilling out over the edges and onto the grass. Panic turned into terror. Gavin screamed.

Scott Cudmore knew he couldn't let this get the better of him but that was difficult. He had to write his reply with tact as he didn't want people to think ill of him if it could affect the children in his care. He knew he couldn't let them talk about Maggie like that though, and so he was working on the perfect comment for the paper's Facebook page when the scream came from the back yard.

"What now?" he said aloud as he recognized the cry as being from the melodramatic Gavin. He hurried to the sliding door and made his way outside to find Samantha holding a screaming Gavin in her arms. She tried to calm him down with soothing words which seemed to be having little to no effect so far.

Scott scanned the area in an attempt to understand what was happening. Gavin's favorite toys were in a hole dug in the sandbox. Lily and Patrick sat back to back like they often did. They sat on the opposite side of the sandbox and while Patrick cocked his head to listen, trying to understand in his own way what was happening. Lily sat quietly staring at a pair of naked Barbie dolls. She had a doll clutched firmly in each hand as she sat in one of her dazes Scott knew so well.

"What's going on?" Patrick asked with childlike inno-
cence, yet sincere concern.

Scott placed a hand on Gavin's shoulder so that the
boy would feel his presence, as that usually helped when
he broke into hysterics.

"Worms!" Gavin screamed as tears gushed and he
clutched his body to Samantha's.

"What's happening?" Patrick asked with growing
panic in his voice.

"Lily," Scott snapped. He could see she was in one of
her usual moods when she retreated into herself and
appeared in a daze. Scott knew the best way to calm Patrick
was with his sister's presence and attention. So this was
not the time for her to retreat into one of her moods. The
four-year-old twins were more than Scott bargained for
and ever since they had moved in, Gavin had become
quite the attention seeker, often going into hysterics for
no apparent reason. The hysterical crying persisted as
Gavin grabbed onto Samantha tighter, climbing up onto
her higher while looking down into the sandbox. His fear
was apparent, though there was nothing there that could
explain this outburst. Scott rubbed Gavin's back with a
gentle up and down motion, trying to calm him.

"Gav, if there was a worm, it is gone now. Look, there
isn't anything in the sandbox anymore except sand and
your toys." Scott said, trying to calm Gavin.

Looking down into the box, Gavin shrieked louder. He
was seeing something that just was not there.

"What's happening? Why is Gavin crying?" Patrick
repeated his question, an alarmed tone in his voice.
Looking back at Lily, Scott saw a large smile on the young
girl's face, her eyes fixated on the sandbox.

"Lily?" Scott repeated a bit louder. This time she
snapped out of the spell she was under and as if by instinct,

she reached behind her and placed a hand on Patrick's arm. She did this without saying a word as Patrick's growing agitated state dissipated.

"Everything is okay, Patrick. Gavin just thought he saw something in the sandbox but it was nothing," Scott said.

Through sobs, Gavin tried to talk. "But...there...is... (sniffles)...look!" Gavin pointed downwards, his cheeks covered in tears.

"Bring him inside, please, Sam?"

Samantha picked up her book which she had dropped near her chair and carried Gavin inside as he clung to her and sobbed into her shoulder.

A bewildered Scott scanned the sandbox and didn't see the worms that had upset Gavin so much. He picked up Patrick and took Lily by the hand and led them inside with the promise of cookies and milk. Patrick smiled at the mention of cookies, but Lily simply followed, her pair of Barbies clutched in her free hand. The sullen little girl glanced back at the sandbox where a small lock of synthetic blonde hair protruded from where she had buried the third Barbie doll. A chilled breeze whipped some of the sand away from the doll as a long slimy worm coiled its body around the Barbie's neck.

Chapter 3
Return to Oakwood Island
June

The disheveled looking Detective Burke had given up. He had been struggling against the wind and rain, his large plastic framed glasses accumulating rain drops, which made things even more difficult as he couldn't see much. He was trying to light his Peter Jackson menthol cigarette but failed every time. His Zippo wouldn't stay lit against the strong, warm southerly winds of the open water as he rode the ferry to Oakwood Island. His cigarette was nearly soaked by the drops of rain that splashed and dissipated onto it. He had already lost his baseball cap as it was blown off his head with an especially strong gust. While lost in his own thoughts, the cap had gone over the rail and into the bay before he was able to process what was happening. He didn't really care as it had clashed with his tie, though it had matched his stained shirt, wrinkled pants and disheveled hair. The mandatory leave of absence from the Anchor's Point Police Department really wasn't agreeing with him and no matter how much he had insisted, both his doctor and the therapist he had been ordered to see weren't ready to let him get back to work.

Between the anxiety brought on by not solving the gruesome island murders five years ago, and the nightmares of a fanged hairy beast stalking him in rooms covered in blood splatter, the detective was a changed man. What had been left of the old sarcastic Burke seemed to be erased when he'd had his heart attack, a little over a year after the death of Officer Ryan McGregor. Once back to work, he was assigned to a desk job. That wasn't something he handled well, either. Stress leave was in his future, even if he wouldn't admit it to himself. He had tried drinking and even failed at that. As it turned out, the detective had developed an intolerance to booze, his body not able to break down alcohol efficiently. He felt like a failure and was ready to give up and take an early retirement. At least he thought he'd been ready until the remains of the botanist Danny Nolan were found on a remote part of Oakwood Island. Even though he was still on leave, Burke insisted on being the one to notify Danny's family and colleagues about the remains found. His psychiatrist agreed, thinking it might bring closure that was needed and may finally be the missing key that would allow Burke to forgive himself for not solving the Oakwood Island cases.

During the primary investigation, a fellow researcher, Jin Hong, had expressed concern when Danny had not gone back to work. When Danny was officially reported as missing, everyone assumed the worst. When his body didn't turn up with the others in the old trailer, his disappearance had remained a mystery. Human remains had then been found deep in the forest on Oakwood Island in April, and just a month later the odd pile of bones had been discovered by the Stuarts. The other detectives and forensic experts were content to wait for the DNA test results, but when Burke had learned that both locations had contained traces of the same plant enzymes, fungus, and animal hairs collected from the original murder scenes, Burke knew the remains belonged to Danny. Burke's obsession returned with a vengeance. It took a lot to convince his friend Harold Randolf, who also happened to be the coroner, to give him a copy of the autopsy report on Danny's remains. Since plant enzymes and fungus were something Jin Hong was more than familiar with, it didn't take long for Burke to send him a copy of the report. Jin theorized that the fungus was something Danny had likely brought with him from the rain forest. The question though remained why? It had made no sense to the fellow researcher. The fact that Danny's body had retained traces of a fungus only previously found in Peru confused Jin enough for him to contact Burke, fueling the fire that had already been reignited with the finding of Danny's remains. With more animal remains found on the island recently containing fresh traces of the plant enzymes and fungus, Burke could not stay away. He had packed a duffel bag with a few changes of clothes, toiletries and put his own case file folders into a box before catching the first ferry to Oakwood Island that same day.

Burke adjusted his large, plastic framed glasses, pulled his cell phone from his pocket and saw a notification of a missed call. With the strong winds from the bay, it was no wonder he hadn't heard his phone ring. With the familiar island in sight, his cell signal was good enough for him to return the call, but first he would need to get out of the wind.

Once in his messy car, Burke lit his menthol cigarette, inhaled deeply and coughed until tears ran down his face. Once he regained his breath, he took another long drag of his cigarette before hitting the dial button returning the missed call.

"You called," Burke said as the call was picked up.

"Are you serious about this or are you fucking with me," Jin Hong blurted.

"Serious about what?"

"The test results from those dead animals found on Oakwood Island. Are they real?" Jin asked.

"Of course they're real," Burke replied as he took a drag from his cigarette. While cradling his phone between his shoulder and ear, the cigarette now between his lips, he shifted his glasses and dug through the box in his passenger seat until he found the folder he wanted. "I mean they better be real. I had to bribe Randolph with a very expensive bottle of scotch." He left out the part about him no longer being able to drink said Scotch as it felt unimportant at the moment.

"The fungus is the same type found on Danny's remains," Jin replied. "Well, a mutated version but close enough that it has to be from the same strain."

"I know," Burke replied as he struggled with the folder, the phone and a lit cigarette. "It's the same shit they found in the animals five years ago, too."

"Not really," Jin replied. "But damned close."

Ignoring the comment, Burke continued. "The same shit that Maggie was infested with. Well similar stuff anyways. We know that now."

"Who?" Jin asked.

"Maggie, the waitress who killed herself by jumping off the roof of the hospital."

"You lost me," Jin replied.

"Never mind that," Burke said as ashes fell from the cigarette into the folder. Burke shook some of the ashes out of it before flopping it back in the box. "What I want to know is does that have anything to do with the half-eaten bodies I can't get out of my head? I can't see how it's connected but I've little else to go on at this point and I'm getting desperate."

"Well you said there were traces of the same stuff at those crime scenes too; the same stuff that was found on Danny's body. It's too bad the chamber maid of the motel threw out those baggies she said were in his room."

"Yeah, well he never came back, so they cleaned the room like they always do. We only know about that because that was the only odd thing she had found in his room when she cleaned it out. That's why she remembered it."

"I'd love to have gotten my hands on those baggies," Jin replied. "But with those new dead animals they found, I'm coming to Oakwood."

"I was hoping you would say that so I wouldn't actually have to come out and ask you to," Burke replied as he dropped what was left of his cigarette into an old coffee cup. It made a hissing sound as it dropped into the cold coffee in the bottom of the cup.

"Maybe you can help me make sense out of all this crap," Burke said as he spotted a familiar man struggling to keep an old, wide brimmed brown hat from blowing off his head. As Burke watched, Jack Whitefeather made his way across the ferry and got into his old, red 1950 Ford truck. Jack looked older than Burke remembered. Perhaps the island was taking its toll on the old Mi'kmaw man as well. Maybe Burke wasn't the only one who couldn't forget those gruesome murders, he thought as he watched Jack.

"I'll talk to Randolf about consulting you on all this," Burke added. "I want it as an official thing, just in case we find something important. I don't want them to dismiss what you find and this way, my name doesn't have to be attached to it either."

"So I take it you're still on sick leave then," Jin stated. "Are you sure you should be doing this?"

"Just try and stop me," Burke replied.

"I'll be there in a few days at the most." Jin replied, thinking it wise not to argue with the stubborn off duty detective. The heart attack had turned Burke into a sour man with little to no patience. While Jin felt like some of the residents of Oakwood Island and that the sudden end to the gruesome murders was a good thing, the detective hated the fact that they remained unsolved. They ended the call after agreeing to meet as soon as Jin Hong set foot on Oakwood Island.

Burke rolled down his window a little bit, adjusted his large glasses and lit another cigarette as he watched Jack with disdain. He wondered how much the mysterious old Mi'kmaw man really knew. What was he not telling the people of Oakwood Island about the events of five years ago?

Jack sat in his old Ford truck, in complete stillness and peaceful quiet as he waited for the ferry to dock on Oakwood Island. In the distance, he watched the beacon of the small lighthouse which was located at the tip of the island. Jack Whitefeather's occasional trips off the island had become more frequent since a cousin on the mainland's First Nations reserve and community had been diagnosed with cancer. Jack would deliver him medicine he grew himself and recommended for the pain. But each time he left, the yearning to return to Oakwood Island grew stronger.

As he waited for the ferry to dock, an old, black-feathered friend landed on the wet hood of his truck, the bird's cawing sounds resonating against the metal of the vehicle. Jack's brow furrowed under the rim of his hat as he spoke.

"What's the matter, you ol' squawker?" Jack asked aloud, knowing full well the bird couldn't hear his voice through the windshield with such strong winds.

The crow seemed agitated as it cawed at him twice more and pecked at the hood of the truck. It cocked its head to the side as if questioning something. Jack had never seen his feathered friend exhibit such strange behavior.

A momentary flash came over Jack as if he was blinded by a bright light. Sensing the crow was trying to tell him something, he locked eyes with the black bird and before he could meditate, the flash came again but this time it lingered, as if latching on. He had spent most of his life looking through the eyes of this crow, but it was always he who initiated the act and not the other way around. This struck Jack as strange.

When the brightness dissipated, he saw himself sitting in the truck. He recognized right away that he was seeing through the eyes of the bird. He could see his tired eyes looking back at the crow as it cawed loudly. It was like looking in a mirror. A chill went through Jack's spine and gooseflesh ran up his arms when he noticed the glow in the passenger seat of the truck. The bright glimmer cast a strange glow onto his own dark skin, shimmering like sunlight on a lake, it reflected on the side of his face. He could almost feel that shimmering light dancing on his own cheek. Moving his attention from his own self onto the source of the light, he noticed that it had a human form to it when the outline of an arm and a hand reached over to try and touch his cheek. This was a familiar human form, he sensed. After a few seconds passed, the shimmer died down and clarity washed over him at once. He reached out his hand towards the woman's form, now clear to him, his voice cracking as he spoke to her.

"Nukumi," Jack uttered. A word spoken in a language he had almost forgotten while living among the white man for so long. *Grandmother.* While the spirit in the truck was of a much younger woman than he had known, he recalled the only picture he had of his grandmother at that age. In the sepia image, her dress was marred by a long scorch mark that started at the lower right bodice and ran up to her left shoulder. Jack had never learned where the strange burn had come from, or why his grandmother wore a dress with such a mark on it. She wore a non-traditional lace ribbon in her hair. This was the exact same image of the spirit with the flickering silver aura he saw sitting next to him in his truck.

The crow cawed once more, awakening Jack from his trance, the reflected image of him and his grandmother's spirit dissipated as fast as it had appeared. As the bird took flight, a horn blared from the car behind his truck as he realized the ferry had docked. He was holding up the other passengers from disembarking. His mind still foggy, he drove off the ferry and onto the island he loved. He pulled into a parking space near the wharf and looked up, watching his black feathered friend fly away into the distance, towards the lighthouse. He stepped out of the truck, standing by the open door as he watched the bird disappear behind the tree line near the rugged and rocky coastline. He couldn't help but feel perplexed by what had just occurred. The bird had initiated sight. Something it had never done. Sure, it had goaded him into paying attention many times. It had done strange things to steer him in directions it thought Jack needed to go, but never had it showed him something using sight without Jack reaching out first.

Jack removed his hat and peered inside his truck through the open door, wondering if the spirit of his grandmother was still there. He had never seen the spirit of his grandmother Sparrow Whitefeather until just now and there had to be a reason for her to have come from her resting place.

For the first time in his life, Jack felt a nervous anxiety towards a spirit he saw through the crow. He had befriended the bird a long time ago. So long ago, in fact, that the crow should be long dead as they don't normally live this long. Jack always assumed his link to the crow somehow added to its longevity. In a vain sort of way, he assumed that the bird would live as long as he was alive. This was a crazy notion, but he had no other explanation as to why this crow had lived so long. It was no ordinary crow, he had always known that. But now, for the first time, he found himself thinking about it, wondering if perhaps there was more to it than he had imagined.

Chapter 4
The Birth of a Curse
Year: 1898

The scorching sun had set over the small, dusty, one-room log cabin over an hour ago, and the baby still hadn't come. The screams that echoed in the somber cabin had started in the early morning hours at sunrise. As the soon-to-be mother struggled with the pain, an omen of what was to come shattered the silence time and again with each contraction she endured. The baby was a month early. A Mi'kmaw woman, who often visited the island to trade her services as a medicine woman and seamstress, had offered to come help with the delivery in exchange for vegetables at harvest time. Although the crops were not doing well due to a severe lack of rain, she had kept her promise and still came around to help in any way she could, as often as possible. With the baby coming earlier than expected though, she hadn't yet been there to offer the help with the delivery she had promised.

When the contractions had come earlier that day, Henri had sent for the Mi'kmaw woman named Sparrow Whitefeather who was on a neighboring farm tending to an ailing elder. Someone had gone to fetch her, but the horse drawn cart had not yet returned with the young woman. It was taking much more time than it should. Time Martha Masterson didn't feel she had at this point as she clutched her husband's hand even harder as she struggled to stand. In the glow of a lantern, Henri Masterson felt his wife's grip get stronger as she screamed again, struggling to take one more step.

In perfect timing with Martha's latest contraction, a woman named Bessie Chapman arrived at the cabin to help the couple. She told Henri that with three children of her own, she would be of assistance to deliver the baby. Henri had not argued. Without Sparrow Whitefeather there to deliver the baby, Henri knew he needed any help he could get. He ushered her in without hesitation.

Martha braced herself on the table as another contraction began. She screamed in agony as the pain spread down throughout her abdomen and back, the mounting pressure of each contraction more unsupportable than the last one. It was more pain than she could have ever imagined. Her hands grabbed the edges of the rough planks, her skinny fingers grasping them so hard that her fingers whitened with the force. Letting go of the table with one hand, she held her belly, cupping it with the length of her right hand and arm, holding it tight. She moaned as she exhaled a deep, slow breath out as the contraction relapsed temporarily. The room swayed around her. Exhausted and dehydrated, she began swaying to her left. Bessie caught her and pulled her up again and leaned her against the table. She knew she had to act fast.

"Help her," the strange woman said to Henri. Her wild eyes saw the pregnant woman's needs with anticipation. It appeared she knew exactly what to say well in advance of when it was needed, where to go well before the steps were expected. *She does know what she is doing*, thought Henri, relieved.

"Help her onto the table," she snapped at Henri as she spread a thick wool blanket over the wooden planks. The long table was assembled from salvaged planks from an old boat. It sat in the center of the room where Martha would give birth to her first child. Henri didn't dare ignore what she told him. Helping his pregnant wife, he draped one of her arms over his shoulders and helped her place her sweat soaked body on the table.

With Henri's help, Martha struggled onto the hard table and collapsed with exhaustion. Bessie placed a few pillows and blankets to support Martha's back. She pulled up Martha into a semi-seated position.

"Come," Bessie urged. "The baby's coming," she stated while helping Martha into a birthing position. She pulled up the folds of Martha's dress and pushed her legs apart. She heard a gasp coming from Henri who stood behind her.

She turned, grasped a nearby wooden pail and handed it to Henri.

"Fetch me some water from the well. Make haste!"

Henri clutched clumsily at the bucket with a confused expression. He looked at his wife, spread out on the table as if seeking her approval for him to do as the woman had asked.

His wife screamed from the pain from yet another contraction and paid no attention to Henri.

"Now!" Bessie shouted at Henri.

An anxious Henri reached for the lantern before realizing that he couldn't take it with him this time. The women needed it more than he did. He paused at the doorway, watching as the strange woman spoke with a firm and loud voice to his wife.

"Good. Now, when I tell you to push, you push."

Henri heard his wife scream as he exited the cabin into the black night. He looked up to find thick clouds covering the moon. This made the evening's darkness even more disheartening and difficult to navigate. Under normal circumstances and with the ability of taking his time, he could have easily found the old well in the absence of light. This year's drought, however, meant that their well had dried up months earlier, forcing Henri to dig a new well further away from their cabin. Even though this well seemed to have plenty of water to last them throughout the driest of years, the fact that it was farther away from the cabin was going to be a challenge with this untimely delivery. He knew he needed to be quick, but not being able to see the path leading to the well proved much more difficult than he expected. Another scream resounded from the small log cabin that he called home. It shook him to the core and made him clutch at the bucket while he strained to see where he stepped, stumbling now and then along the path, his old boots catching roots and rocks as he went along. Eventually, his eyes adjusted to the darkness as he made his way to the new well.

The young woman named Sparrow had argued that she could get to the Masterson's cabin faster on foot, but the large, bearded man would hear nothing of it. He had insisted on taking her on the horse drawn cart, arguing with her that riding would be best and that he would get her there without delay. Sparrow had felt an unease wash over her as she conceded and agreed to go by the horse drawn cart.

The baby was much too early and this worried the doula. She had seen this before and Sparrow thought that perhaps her estimation had been wrong. She had felt confident earlier in Martha's pregnancy that she knew when the child would be born. But as the mother's belly had grown large faster than anticipated, Sparrow couldn't help but think that she might have been wrong this time, even though the moon counts since the woman's last period should have brought her delivery at the end of another full month. Sparrow's instincts were always accurate, having been a doula since she'd been a young girl, helping her mother in her own duties and learning the ways from her, so this unexpected early birth concerned her. With clouds parting and the light of the moon helping, the bearded man pushed his horse harder. Sparrow held onto her seat next to the man, holding on tight to her basket with the supplies she would need to deliver the premature baby. In his careless haste, the man continued to push the horse, bellowing his thunderous voice to order the animal to go faster still. As they rounded a sharp turn, the cart hit a large rock and broke a wheel. The horse neighed as its reigns were pulled back by the stopped cart. Without hesitation, Sparrow jumped off the cart, grabbed her basket, tore a slit in her dress and ran in the direction of the cabin she had visited so often in the last few months.

Soon the beacon of the small lighthouse appeared in the distance. She knew she was close. She ran faster still until she could see the cabin on the horizon and a small glow emanated from the open door. As she ran toward the wooden cabin, eager to help deliver the Masterson's baby, she noticed a woman heading into the forest on the opposite side of the home. Confused at first, she slowed her pace. The running woman was not Martha, she was much too mobile for that. She ran fast with long silver hair trailing out behind her. As she watched the woman vanish into the woods beyond the small home, Sparrow hesitated, as she somehow knew the woman didn't belong there. An anguished bawl scream coming from the shack made her decision for her and her legs carried her towards the man's voice. She heard panic in his cries as she made her way to the path, then through the doorway, stepping over a wet floor and a half full bucket of water.

Martha lay on the blood covered table, her legs spread and half a baby protruding from her vaginal opening. Her labia had been torn several inches and she was bleeding profusely. The baby was half out and seemed stuck as Martha was too weak to push; she drifted in and out of consciousness. Henri, screaming and in hysterics, was standing at the end of the table, his hands and upper arms covered in blood as he tried to hold the slippery baby.

Without hesitation, Sparrow stepped in front of Henri, shoving him out of the way as she took over. Knowing how to grip the baby with her right hand and where to push down on the mother's belly, she helped free the baby. As she handed it to a stunned Henri, she wiped her bloody hands on her dress and removed her apron. Using this, she pushed it against Martha's labia in hopes of stopping the bleeding. She had believed it to be a tear at first, but now could clearly see the woman had been cut with a knife. She was also hemorrhaging. This was bad, very bad. Sparrow knew time was of the essence, but tried to remain calm. The first few moments of a baby's birth would mark the path of its life and would determine if it was to be full of chaos and fear, or one of calm and peace.

"Bring her the baby, Henri. Let him meet his mother." Sparrow's voice cracked as she tried to hide her own fear.

"Martha," Henri muttered. "It's a boy. Martha?" He approached his wife, carrying the small baby in his large, burly hands.

Martha lifted her head from the table, her eyes trying to adjust and look at her husband as she spoke. Her skin was akin to February snow.

"What about the other one?" Martha croaked, her voice parched and dry.

"What?" Henri asked in confusion. "I don't understand,

Martha." He looked back at Sparrow, who lifted her face from her task of trying to stop the bleeding, and looked puzzled also.

"Twins, Henri. We had two babies," Martha added as she held up a trembling hand toward the baby her husband cradled.

"Twins?" Sparrow inquired. "There's only one child, Martha."

"There were two," Martha added. "Bessie has the other."

Sparrow's eyes grew wide as she realized that Bessie must have been the woman she had seen running into the woods. There was no other baby to be seen in the cabin. Twins would explain the rapid growth of Martha's belly. But the other baby, Bessie must have taken it. *Why*, wondered Sparrow.

"Hold this and press as much as possible. Don't take the pressure off," she said as she showed Henri the crumpled apron she had been using to stem Martha's bleeding. Once Henri held both the cloth and the baby, Sparrow walked over to the doorway, picked up the axe that was leaning against the door frame and ran from the cabin heading in the direction she had seen the woman go.

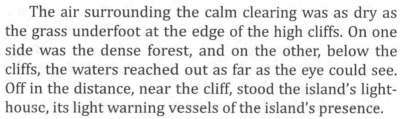

The air surrounding the calm clearing was as dry as the grass underfoot at the edge of the high cliffs. On one side was the dense forest, and on the other, below the cliffs, the waters reached out as far as the eye could see. Off in the distance, near the cliff, stood the island's lighthouse, its light warning vessels of the island's presence.

During overcast nights like this, darkness carried itself on the slick surface of the water as much as it did below. The beacon of the lighthouse provided but a very faint glow on the surrounding land as it made its circular sweep.

Bessie had set the newborn baby down on a patch of dirt as soon as she had come out of the forested area. She had run as fast as she could to get to the clearing, where the wide pentagram she had previously carved into the soil waited eagerly for its infant adornment.

With blood covered hands and forearms, the tall, grey-haired woman picked up a large, sharpened human shoulder blade taken from a small pile nearby. Bessie began cleaning the deep grooves in the soil, fixing what had been disturbed, remaking the lines of the five pointed star, digging with the bone to ensure its trenches were deep and clear of debris. Directly in the center of the large pentagram, lay the naked baby girl, still covered in birthing liquids and blood, awaiting her fate. Her cries became louder as Bessie took a small, wooden kerosene bucket that she had hidden in the brush and set it on the edge of the pentagram. She turned the spout at the base of the bucket, allowing its contents to flow. Soon, a strong pungent and oily odour drifted around the area as the liquid filled the channels in the soil. Bessie stepped inside the center of the pentagram where the baby kicked and screamed. With a few strikes, Bessie lit a match and set the kerosene on fire, creating flames in the pentagram that burned a foot tall.

The small baby kicked her tiny newborn legs and scratched the air with her small arms. Her newborn's lungs inhaled the reek and stench of the burning kerosene, making her cough and cry so hard she choked as she screamed louder still.

Reaching into the small pile of human bones, Bessie picked up a smaller rib bone. With intricate markings on its length and the end having been sculpted as sharp as a knife blade, Bessie's eyes widened as she grasped the handle of the makeshift dagger. She spoke in a tongue that didn't belong on this island as she ran the sharpened bone across the palm of her left hand, drawing blood.

The winds that had been calm picked up strength, fanning the flames that burned all around the baby, making them climb higher into the darkness. In the baby's eyes, the fiery light danced, reflections of all that was to come. All around them, dust began rising with each gust as Bessie lifted one bloody hand into the sky and placed the other on the baby's head. She spoke her incantation, calling forth words that no woman from this island should know, though she spoke them with confidence. She raised the sharpened bone high as she repeated the peculiar words, the flames danced in her wide eyes too as they stared into the sky above, looking at the darkness and beyond.

The winds grew stronger still and began to stir the leaves of the trees nearby. A few loose branches flew about, some flying over the cliff side and being carried down into the churning waters. The baby lay quiet now, its eyes opened wide as if staring up in the sky, the flames warming her blood-slicked body. Above the baby and Bessie, high in the night sky, a crow cawed. It swooped around swaying trees a few times before making its way over the pentagram. It darted this way and that, flying in the same pattern that burned on the ground below.

Sparrow ran as fast as she could into the woods, in the same direction she'd seen the woman with the grey hair flee. The axe was heavy to carry, but she had known by instinct to bring it. Her arms and legs shook as she ran but finding and safely bringing home the newborn baby kept her running. The small trail in the wooded area near the cabin was slight but she knew how to keep her footing in such terrain. She was used to the forest.

The trees ahead of her thinned and she saw light coming from flames. Gripping the axe with a stronger hold in her left hand, she ran harder, her legs pumping and her heartbeat quickening with each step. She felt the air surrounding her change as she got closer. It became heavy, like the muggy blanket of air right before a huge rainstorm.

Sparrow emerged from the forest and into the clearing to see Bessie sitting in a ring of fire as she raised her hand into the air. Winds whipped about dust and leaves, creating a swirling vortex of debris. Sparrow saw something clutched in the woman's hand as it shone dully in the firelight. Blood covered the woman's hands and trickled down her arm where the object she clutched pierced the skin of her hand. Without hesitation, Sparrow jumped through the flames and struck Bessie with the butt of the axe, knocking her to the side and into the fire in the process. Looking down at her feet, Sparrow gasped as she saw something she didn't expect to see. The baby girl. Though covered in blood, the infant was still alive. Sparrow had feared the worst when she had seen the weapon in the woman's hand and the blood trickling down her arm. The baby lay quietly as she wriggled about amongst the hot, crackling flames. All around them, the winds grew stronger, whipping about loose forest debris in a slow but very odd sort of orchestrated swirling pattern around them.

Sparrow dropped the axe and scooped up the slippery child. She cradled her against her left shoulder as she stepped out of the burning pentagram, her dress singed at the hem in the process. She patted her dress to make sure it would not catch flame with one hand, while she struggled to hold onto the baby. Once sure her dress was not catching fire, she turned her back to the diminishing flames to get a good look at the baby girl. She pulled her up and away from her shoulder, holding her with both hands, trying to examine her body, looking for visible wounds or any sign of an injury. The small baby girl, wide-eyed but calm, seemed fine, other than being covered with her mother's blood.

A shadow appeared over the baby's face, and Sparrow realized that she had not struck Bessie as hard as she thought. Clutching the baby to her chest, she spun around to come face to face with the crazed woman. The woman's dress was on fire.

Bright flames were spreading from the bottom of her dress and creeping upwards as smoke curled about her. Her bloody hands tried to grab the child from Sparrow's protective embrace.

"Give her to me now," Bessie cried as she clutched for the newborn. "You don't know what you're doing."

"No," Sparrow shouted, her voice filled with fear. "You'll hurt her."

The women grappled. Sparrow held the baby close to her shoulder as she struggled against the woman. Bessie appeared frightened, although she was the one causing this chaos. Bewildered by the actions of this woman, Sparrow took several steps away from the remnants of the burning pentagram on the cliff's edge. The woman followed her, pleading as she went.

"Please, give her to me. I need her!" Bessie wailed.

"No! Get away!" Sparrow replied, gripping the newborn tighter.

"You must give her to me. She told me what I had to do. Please, you must!" The flames on Bessie's skirt were now up to her knees. She appeared unphased by the tendrils of smoke and the flames growing larger.

"Who told you? Who are you speaking of?" Sparrow cried out. She knew she had to protect the baby.

"The voice in the field. She told me what I had to do! You cannot stop me from doing what I need to do! Give me the baby!" Bessie's dress was engulfed with flames from the waist down yet she seemed completely unaffected.

The winds grew even stronger as Sparrow stepped dangerously close to the edge of the cliff, trying to protect the child as best as she could. The slowly churning vortex of debris from earlier was now being transformed into a windstorm that Sparrow had never seen the likes of until tonight. Branches and twigs flung outwards and in all directions. The dust and grit hit her cheeks and she tried to shield her and the baby's eyes. With each plea from Bessie the gusts of wind grew stronger.

"You are not hurting this child!" Sparrow shouted.

"You don't understand," Bessie replied. "If I don't sacrifice this newborn child, we will all die."

"You've lost your mind." Sparrow continued backing away from the woman, scared for herself but more so for the baby she held and was desperately trying to protect.

"She will come and make it rain. She's told me so. She promised me she would. Our crops will grow, and we will flourish. All of us."

"What?" Sparrow replied as she stepped next to an oak tree that had its roots embedded in the cliff's edge.

The winds grew wild, the flames in the pentagram flickered stronger as the women argued, unbeknownst to them that they debated not only the fate of the child, but of the oak tree covered island as well.

"Give her to me," Bessie cried as she lunged at the woman with sharpened bone in hand. The flames of her dress were now burning higher, and the sleeves were starting to catch fire. Sparrow stepped to the side, avoid-

42

ing the crazed woman's desperate grasp. Bessie nearly lost her balance, almost toppling over the cliff, but instead she grasped at the tree and stopped herself from falling to her death.

Bessie turned to face Sparrow as she spoke. "You don't understand," she pleaded with everything she had left inside; tears streaked her face as she attempted to convince Sparrow to give up the baby. "She has to die for the rest of us to live."

In that moment, the strong winds blew in their direction. Several pieces of dry and dead branches, crisp old leaves as well as twigs rushed towards them in a gust. Both of their skirts flapped back and forth, getting caught in the crosswinds that were blowing from the land and the sea. Bessie's grey hair flew out behind her, as the strongest gust caught the edge of the cliff. Bessie's eyes widened as she peered down in time to see the oak tree's roots give way and her dress engulfed in flames. Lifting her head, she locked eyes with Sparrow's, her mouth unable to produce any sounds with the dreaded fear that engulfed her. She looked down in panic as the earth under the mighty tree's roots began to crumble. Bessie struggled to keep her footing but stumbled as the dirt beneath her feet fell away, bit by bit, as it parted from its hold on the cliff and began its descent in a slow, but downward slide.

Sparrow turned her back to the woman, unable to watch the scene unfolding before her, and trying to protect the baby now not from any imminent danger, but from the emotional scars that would mark the child all of its life.

As Bessie stumbled backward, she flung the sharpened bone towards Sparrow with as much force as possible. Sparrow cried out in pain as the sharpened bone pierced her back and protruded from her right shoulder.

Stumbling forward, Sparrow fell to her knees, but

managed to not drop the infant despite the unbearable pain in her shoulder. She then set the child on the soft, grassy earth, fearing that she might drop the baby in her current state.

Sparrow turned her head to see the tree tumbling out of sight and over the edge of the cliff. A large section of the earth around it had also slid away. On the new edge of the cliff, Bessie's fingers desperately grasped at the dirt and dry grass, trying to clamber back to solid ground. But the grass was dry from the drought, and the roots were not as strong as they would have been in a normal summer. As Bessie's hands failed to find a solid hold, more earth crumbled away. Her scream was carried to Sparrow by the strong winds, a scream that she would never forget, and neither would the small child, even if only remembered in her nightmares.

Many years later, once the shock had worn off and the deep cut from the sharpened bone had finally stopped hurting, Sparrow would tell the tale of how the island and the oak tree itself had protected the child from a certain death. The island covered in oak trees, full of their protective energy; the same island that would eventually bear the fitting name of Oakwood.

Her flaming dress now extinguished by the seawater, Bessie waited. She hoped and prayed that Sparrow would dare to step onto the new edge of the cliff to see, by the faint glow of the lighthouse beacon, her body on the rocks below. Next to her, half in the water was the oak tree, decimated with broken branches floating off in every direction and its dead leaves carried by the waves into the surrounding darkness.

She knew that even if she was seen by Sparrow, that the native woman couldn't have seen that Bessie was still alive, not from this distance and in the dark of night. Her body lay battered with several broken bones and she was unable to move her arms or legs. Bessie coughed hard. Spatters of blood sprayed the front of her blackened dress and down back onto her face as she looked up helplessly at the ridge of the cliff. She watched for the woman who had stopped her attempt to save her family from starvation. She thought of her children, already so frail and small. The youngest always sick from a lack of nutrition. She had been desperate to save them, to feed them the food their bodies needed to sustain them. The food that had become so hard to grow since the drought had come.

Each year, less and less rain had fallen, and the crops had been scarce. On the third year, the drought that had plagued the island seemed to have gotten worse, but Bessie had figured out how to make the rains come again.

Drifting in and out of consciousness, she recalled what she had been told by the voice of the woman she had called upon, late one night in the dried-up fields. The woman's voice in the darkness had said she would help the rains come, but only if she sacrificed a human life. Bessie knew there was still time left in the growing season and that she could save her family. She believed the voice that had come to her. She had no other choice. Ignoring it would mean sure death for her children and herself. However, she now knew that death was coming for her, and soon, as pain racked her body with each agonizing gasp for breath. The taste of blood was overwhelming in her mouth and in the back of her throat. Her chest burned as hot as the flames she had ignited mere minutes earlier. As much as she tried to remember the faces of her children, the noises surrounding her seemed to edge those thoughts out.

The wind howled in her ears, driving the waves that lapped at the bloody rocks she lay upon, sending cold seawater over her body, keeping her conscious. Keeping her in pain. The burns she had suffered from her flaming dress were now felt. Pieces of her skin floated in the sea. Her exposed flesh, burned and charred seared with pain from the salty water.

As she opened her eyes, she saw a shimmer of light flickering above the cliff's edge. Her pentagram still burned.

A crow fluttered down from the cliffs above and landed on the rocks near her. The blackness of the bird made it hard to see as it cocked its head and looked at the broken body on the rocks. With a quick flutter of its wings, the crow landed on Bessie's chest.

"No," Bessie muttered. She coughed blood before she spoke again. "I did what you asked... no!" She spoke to the bird as if somehow it could deliver this message; a message that no longer needed to be relayed because she had failed.

The crow cawed at the sky before pecking out one of Bessie's eyes and swallowing it whole. Bessie tried to scream but only coughed. Blood speckled the crow's plumage, tiny beads of dark crimson splattering its feathers and beak. She tried to swat at the crow, but her arm wouldn't move. As Bessie lay paralyzed on the jutting sea rocks, the crow pecked out her remaining eye as darkness enveloped her. The last thing she felt was cold seawater splashing her face as she heard the crow caw before it lifted itself from her chest and flapped its wings as it took flight.

In the darkness near the sea, a large wave crashed over the rocks and the badly broken body. When the water receded again exposing the rocks, Bessie was gone.

Upon arriving at the cabin with the baby girl in her arms, Sparrow found Henri sitting on a home-made wooden chair. He was sobbing while clutching his new-born son to his body. Sparrow glanced over the room and into Martha's empty gaze. She knew the cut had been too deep. Martha's blood had pooled on and under the table. She gathered a clean blanket from the bed, wrapping the baby girl and placing her in the simple wooden cradle that had been set up weeks ago, in anticipation of the baby's arrival.

Turning her back to him, Henri jumped up when he saw the bone protruding from her shoulder blade.

"You're injured! Who did this?" He shifted his pain and focused his attention on her. "I need to remove it, Sparrow."

She turned her head and nodded.

"That woman did, the one that helped deliver the babies..." Her voice trailed off as Henri began to remove the carved bone, shaped like a dagger. Wincing from the pain, Sparrow took a few deep breaths as Henri cleaned the wound and covered it. Once he was done, she walked over to the table and picked up one of the wool blankets that was on the floor nearby. She closed Martha's eyelids and pulled the blanket over her cold and stiffening body.

"Henri. Give me the boy. He will find comfort with his sister."

Henri looked up at her, his eyes searching hers for some kind of answer, some sort of comfort. Sparrow knew she could never provide him with the answers he deserved, but she promised herself in that instant that she would never stop trying.

"Please, Henri. I want to help him. I want to help you." His tears returned as he handed over the newborn to her.

He put his hands up to his face, sobbing hard. She carried the boy twin to the bed, where she swaddled him in a blanket, trying to keep him warm. Placing him next to his twin sister in the wooden cradle, both babies cooed at each other as they gazed into their eyes for the first time. A calmness spread over Sparrow that she had not felt in a long time, especially not tonight. She pulled a small wool blanket that was at the foot of the cradle to cover both babies and turned to face Henri.

"I know you are heartbroken. But these babies need you, Henri."

He raised his head to meet her gaze.

"Do you know why that woman took your child?"

Henri stared beyond her, at the outline of his wife's body laying cold on their table. He shook his head no.

She thought about what to tell him. He had been through so much already. She did not want to add to his worries and trauma, but she wanted to know if Henri knew why the woman had tried to steal his baby.

"She stole your baby girl, Henri. She ran off with her into the woods. For whatever the reason, she wanted her. I managed to get her back though, and your babies are both safe now."

Sparrow examined Henri who showed no sign of knowing anything about the mad woman's motives.

Henri looked at the cradle, where the twins were sleeping peacefully. He turned back to look at Sparrow and asked with a hint of worry in his voice.

"What if she comes back? I don't know that I can stop her. I don't know how I can take care of these babies without…" His eyes welled up with tears as he looked towards the table where his dead wife was covered. Sparrow took one of Henri's large hands in both of hers as she spoke.

"She will not be coming back. That I am certain, Henri."

She stared at him with a serious look. He nodded his understanding.

Henri, clearly in shock, couldn't take care of the babies in his state. She suggested he go to the nearest neighbour, the one that had come to fetch her with his horse and wagon. She offered to clean up the babies, but most importantly, the pool of blood on and under the table. Henri agreed and stumbled outside, not able to stand the heavy unease of death in his home. The death of his beloved.

It was the next morning before Sparrow noticed the burn mark on the front of her dress. The darkened patch began at her left breast and reached her shoulder. This burn mark confused her. She couldn't recall fire having singed anything other than the hem of her dress. What confused her even more was Bessie. The white woman had been performing what looked to be some sort of devil-worshiping ritual and wanted to kill an innocent baby. A baby who was now motherless and with a father who blamed himself for Martha's death.

When Henri returned home it was almost mid-morning. Although he seemed less in shock than the night before, she knew he had not slept much, if at all. Sparrow wanted to talk to Henri, to try to get a better understanding of why Bessie did what she did. She also feared that she would be blamed, as Bessie was white and she wasn't.

She also knew that only Henri could ever know the real events of that evening, as she felt he deserved the truth. Henri was in a fragile state, though, and so she knew she had to be careful to not make matters worse.

Henri sat down in the wooden chair and looked at Sparrow.

"Where are they?" he said without expression.

"The babies are sleeping." Sparrow replied. "Henri, I think we should talk about last night."

"What is there to talk about? My wife is dead, Sparrow. My babies have no mother." His voice was flat.

She wondered how much she should tell him about what Bessie had done. She knew he was in a fragile emotional state. She didn't want to upset him, but she needed to understand why Bessie had tried to kill one of the infants in some sort of ritual. She worried perhaps there was more to this than just Bessie. Worry drove her to speak to Henri about the matter. Hesitant, she approached him where he sat, eyes sullen with dark circles below them.

"I want to know if you know why Bessie would try to take one of the babies."

"How should I know why? I didn't even know she took one of them until you told me she had."

"She was going on and on about having to take her and that someone had told her she had to do it. Do you know who she was talking about, Henri?"

"I don't know, I don't know who would say such things to her. All I know is that if that crazy woman or anyone else comes near me or my children again..." Henri's voice trailed off as he turned his back to her. "Why did I trust her? I trusted her blindly. She brought about evil in my home, and I welcomed her in..." Henri's voice grew louder.

"Henri, you had no way of knowing what would happen. No way of knowing she would do the things she did!"

"What exactly did she do, Sparrow?" Henri asked.

"Henri, I don't know that we need to go into the details of what happ—" Sparrow was interrupted by Henri's booming voice.

"WHAT did she DO?" he demanded.

"She had a symbol, in the ground, and she had set it ablaze. She had put the baby in the center and she was speaking words I've never heard before. She seemed to be going mad, or she was possessed by the devil." Sparrow felt she had told him too much, as she saw Henri's face turn red and his lips pressed together. He was taking deep breaths, trying to calm himself down. She tried to change the course of their conversation. Sparrow swallowed hard before her next question.

"Was Bessie ever around Martha before yesterday? Did she perhaps mention anything of the sort while she was here?"

Henri slammed his fist down on the table hard, waking the newborns in their cradle. They began to cry.

"I don't know, Sparrow! Don't you understand, I don't know who Bessie is or why she wanted the babies! I just know Martha is gone and it's all my fault."

The babies were crying louder in the small cabin. Their shrill cries intensified as the two spoke, the tension mounting within the walls of the home. "I should never have let her in this house. If only I hadn't, Martha, my beautiful Martha, would still be here." His expression turned to anguish, as he continued blaming himself for his wife's death.

"It's not your fault, Henri." Sparrow tried her best but Henri was not hearing her. His thoughts were fixated on blaming himself. Sparrow knew she would not get answers from Henri. If he had known something, anything, he surely would have told her by now. She tried to console him, to explain that it wasn't his fault.

"I never should have let that insane woman near my Martha. It is all my fault and you can't say otherwise. It was my job to protect her, to help her. I...failed her." His voice trailed as his eyes glanced back to the table where his wife had been murdered less than twelve hours earlier. Though the blood was gone, the stains on the table and floor would remain forever, a constant reminder of his loss.

With time, it became less a point of focus, but every once in a while, he would notice the stain and his jaw would harden. No tears would flow, his anger with himself much too strong to allow that to happen.

As the news of Martha's death and the twins' birth spread, Sparrow altered the tale she told the locals so they wouldn't try to blame her. She felt that she owed the truth to Henri, for having failed to save his wife. She was the one who was supposed to be there to help deliver the babies. But the rest of the people of the island would never be completely convinced that Bessie had been the one doing the devil's work. They would blame her, this she knew. So she had made up a story about Bessie and how she had tried to run for help but that she had stumbled and fallen over the cliff. The island residents believed her story and mourned the loss of Martha as a community.

Sparrow had made sure to leave out the part to both Henri and the islanders about how she thought the island itself had caused the tree to fall and had taken Bessie with it. She also omitted her belief that the island itself had protected the child. This tale she would only tell her own daughter, eventually but this wouldn't be for a long time yet.

Chapter 5
Lurking in the Darkness
Late June

On her day off from work at the hospital, Miriam sat at the kitchen table peeling potatoes while Bradley and Samantha helped by peeling carrots, turnips, and onions. The kitchen in mid-morning was bright with natural light coming from the large windows and sliding patio doors. This room was always full of life. It was the center of the home's main activities, be it with meal preparation, eating, homework or playing board games. It was always full of lively discussions and laughter and that was why it was Miriam's favorite room in their house.

For the first time this summer, Miriam had opened all the windows in the kitchen, as the weather had at last warmed up enough to do so. The three of them peeled, sliced and diced to make scalloped potatoes, stew and shepherd's pie; meals for the next few days.

Scott had taken three of the more energetic foster kids with him to get haircuts and run errands. Plus he wanted Clay, Peter and Colin to go with him to the library. Scott had promised Samantha he'd get her a few books she wanted, including the next in the Potter series. He had taken the boys in hopes of getting them to read more instead of playing video games all the time. That left the three youngest kids at home along with the two eldest who were helping their foster mom with meal prep.

"Hi, Patrick," Miriam said as she noticed her smart little boy, walking into the kitchen, his left hand following the wall, as usual. He was abnormally bright for his age. "Did you want to help us prep?" Miriam's smile was obvious in her voice, the soft tone of her words such a delight to the kids ears. Hearing her talk was almost as nice as the long, loving hugs she often took the time to give to each of them.

"No, mommy. I'm just looking for a puzzle. The one with the animals and trucks and cars." He approached the table with a slow and steady step. Miriam got up from her chair and looked down at him. She brought her face closer to his. She peered into the large sunglasses and saw her own reflection in them, a funny and distorted image of herself, a bit like the fun mirrors at the carnival.

"I'll get it for you, sweetie." Her voice was soft and this made Patrick smile. Unlike others, his foster mom was very soft-spoken around him. She knew loud voices could sometimes upset him due to his keen sense of hearing. She always made sure to speak with a soft tone with him, and this he appreciated, in his own four-year-old way.

Opening the pantry, she bent down and sorted through a large basket with several puzzle boxes, board games and various decks of cards. Finding what she was searching for, she pulled it out and brought it over to Patrick.

"Here you go, kiddo." Patrick reached out and with his fingers he found the edge of the puzzle board. He took it in his arms and turned around.

Once he made his way back, Patrick sat in the middle of the living room, still finding comfort behind his large sunglasses. He placed the large wooden toy puzzle board down in front of him. The board had various shapes cut out where puzzle pieces fit, pieces that had shapes of animals and things with Braille words written on each piece. Patrick took a piece from the pile, felt its shape and proceeded to feel the board to find its place.

His twin sister Lily stood at the window sill, playing with a dismembered Barbie doll. The doll's arms and legs were scattered on the sill while Lily tried to comb the doll's matted hair. Gavin played on the couch. His toy dump truck and toy loader were busy moving pretend gravel. He mimicked scooping it up with the loader, dumping it into the truck and moving it from one side to the other all while making his best impression of the roar of engines.

Lily put her small hand to the window pane as she looked outside, watching the man on the roof on the house across the street. The house had been empty for months. The last occupants, an elderly couple, had only lived there for three weeks when poor old Mr. Ketchum died of a sudden heart attack. A week after that, his wife, Mrs. Ketchum had a stroke. The house had been for sale since. Today there was someone working on redoing the roof. Lily, only four years old, didn't quite understand all that. What she did remember was watching the ambulance take Mr. Ketchum on a stretcher. That had been an exciting day. She also remembered the day Mrs. Ketchum ran outside. She had burst through the front door while Lily stood at the same exact spot she did now, watching and smiling. Mrs. Ketchum had run as fast as her old arthritic-filled legs had allowed her. She had stopped midway on the sidewalk, only to spin around and stare at the two story house. Lily remembered watching for a moment before Mrs. Ketchum slowly fell on her side. She lay in the grass for a long time as Lily watched. Eventually Scott had come to see what had Lily so wrapped up, but it had been too late. Mrs. Ketchum had suffered a stroke and was pronounced dead by the paramedics upon their arrival.

Today she watched as the man on the roof worked. Lily didn't really understand exactly what he was doing.

He sure did make a lot of noise with all the banging he was doing with the big hammer he was using. She knew he was working because he had tools; real ones and not toys. She wondered if today would be another exciting day too.

Ben Augustine's favorite class in high school had been shop. Mostly it had been the carpentry portion of shop class. Ben loved to make things with his hands especially since he found meaning in it. He wanted to give a new life to the trees that had been cut and for their spirit to carry on. His grandfather had taught him that everything in nature has a spirit and that it must be honored, always. The idea that he could both honor the tree's spirits and create something that could help serve his fellow man in different ways was a calling that came to Ben at a young age.

College wasn't something he had thought about while going to school, but he had since learned that to become a carpenter, he would need to complete an apprenticeship. With the completion of a carpenter program at a college though, it would reduce the time required to complete the apprenticeship. Sure, he could learn a lot on his own, and he had done so, but you couldn't list YouTube on a resume as a reference or experience. These days, most people wanted you to have related work experience or technical training in the field before they took you on as an apprentice. In order to make money to go to college, Ben had taken a job with a local sawmill. He had started as a laborer and had since gained the confidence of his boss by always being punctual, doing the job to the best of his abilities and treating everyone with respect. These were the qualities, he learned, that were appreciated in the workforce and rewarded. His boss took notice and he was the one who convinced him to go to college.

"Learn as much as you can and then make sure you come back," he had said to Ben. "My brother has a construction company and he is always looking for carpenters. In the meantime though, maybe I can give him your name if you want to do some other jobs to make more cash for school?" Ben had agreed.

He had continued working at the mill, but he was also doing some side jobs and projects whenever he was needed. On this day, he had been asked to put new shingles on the roof of the old Ketchum house.

Ben had spent the day stripping off the old shingles and was now on the front side of the house, prepping it for the new roofing. It had taken him longer than he had hoped due to the three dormers on the front of the house.

Stripping the old roofing around these without damaging the siding or the windows had been tedious. Ben was now down to the last bits of roofing which were in front of the dormers. Crouched, he struggled with his safety harness while getting ready to pry the bits of roofing off. He had to be careful not to damage the existing flashing like he had been told. Damaging that would mean removing the siding and that was not part of the job. Sure, they would fix it at no extra charge if he did damage the aluminum material that stopped the water from getting in under the siding and into the house, but it would be best if they didn't need to do that.

Ben crouched and carefully pried away a piece of roofing. As he bent down though, something caught the corner of his eye in the window of the dormer where he was working. A glint of something inside the house, he thought. Or maybe merely a reflection in the glass as it was dark in the house. It gave the glass a slight mirrored effect. Nobody was living there, so that was the likely cause of the glint he thought he saw.

He glanced behind him to see what the source of the reflection might have been only to be reminded that he was three stories high. The dormer was in the attic of a two story house which meant he was much higher than he remembered. This thought sent his empty hand to the buckle of his safety harness. Once he was confident it was still secure, he turned his attention back to the task at hand. Before he was able to reach for the strip of roofing, he noticed something in the shadows of the attic. Something definitely moved, he thought.

Before he was able to finish processing that he had seen movement, out of the shadows inside the house, on the other side of the window, a small red ball appeared on the floor of the attic. Focusing his gaze away from inside the house and to his own reflection, he saw the fear in his face and realized he had been holding his breath. Letting out a long breath, his mind started racing with questions. He knew the house was supposed to be empty. He wondered if there was anyone possibly squatting inside the vacant home.

Before he could give it much more thought, a second red ball appeared next to the first just outside the shadows, resting on the floor of the vacant house. Ben shifted his weight, grasped at his safety harness while clutching at the metal pry bar he had been using to remove the shingles. Before he could assess the situation, a third red ball emerged from the shadows of the dark attic, hovering in the air. His breathing was now coming in short, shallow gasps, and he felt a powerful tightening as he watched this red mass hovering approximately five feet off the ground. Confused, and feeling the adrenaline racing through his body, Ben started to rise from the crouched position then wobbled on the sloped roof as he almost lost his footing. He staggered slightly but steadied himself. Just beneath the floating red ball, Ben saw a set of bright white teeth materialize out of thin air, grinning like the Cheshire Cat, but with a crueller twist.

"A fucking clown," he uttered as he took an involuntary step back from his old childhood phobia. The phobia that had been implanted by that stupid movie he had watched when he was way too young to watch such stuff. As he took the step, he suddenly realized that he was near enough to the edge of the roof already that his foot had nothing to land on. He flung his arms out to steady himself but it was too late. Falling backwards, he realized that his safety harness was clipped into a line that was too long, but in that instant, it was too late to do anything about it.

For a few brief moments, he felt himself free-falling, straight down, but as he struggled in his panic, his body turned a bit to the left. The fall came to an abrupt stop. He felt and heard a loud snap when the end of the line was reached. The pain and the pressure on his spine too much for his body to endure caused Ben to pass out. His body dangled alongside the siding of the house, where he would remain for almost an hour.

The angle of the fall, with the line wrapped around his waist, as well as the sudden jarring impact would be explained as the reason for the back injury he would sustain. This was the day that changed the course of his life forever. Soon doctors would tell him they were not sure if the damage to his spinal column would be reparable. One thing they knew for certain, though, was that his dream of becoming a carpenter would never come to be.

Lily stood at the window, the now headless torso of the Barbie doll in one hand and the doll's head in the other. She stood there, silent as she watched Ben dangling from a line off the house across the street. She was completely unaware of the curse that she had inherited from her mother, but she knew if she focused hard enough, she could make things happen. She didn't know how. She had no way of knowing that she made people see things that would scare them, things that would be disturbing to them. All she knew was that when she tried, she could scare people and she liked it. *It's fun to scare people*, thought Lily, as she watched the man she had just scared now dangling from a rope. A giggle escaped her as she continued to watch him.

"Oh my GOD!" Samantha exclaimed as she stood behind Lily. Samantha, while checking on the kids, saw Ben dangling on his safety line. Ben's harness had held him but the way he dangled, bent backwards like he was, it had to be bad, she thought.

A clatter startled Samantha and she heard a scream from behind her. She turned to see that Patrick had dumped his puzzle pieces and was starting his puzzle all over again. The scream had been from Gavin as the puzzle pieces clattering onto the floor had apparently scared him. Gavin, toy truck in hand, stood quivering in fear as he looked outside the window and noticed the hurt man across the street.

"Call 911," Samantha blurted to Miriam. "Tell them someone needs help at the old Ketchum house."

Samantha walked over to Gavin where he stood, terrified. She took his hand and led him away from the frightening scene in the window. Miriam ran to get the cordless phone in the hallway. With the phone in hand she called 911 as she went outside and made her way towards the Ketchum house.

"Lily," Patrick said as he cocked his head to the side in an attempt to hear his twin sister. "Stop it, Lily."

Lily smirked as she dropped the head of the Barbie doll on the floor while watching what was happening at the Ketchum house. She placed her small, bare foot on the head of the doll and slowly put her weight on it, crushing the plastic toy with her heel. Barbie's face, distorted and disfigured stared out with plastic painted eyes underfoot.

Patrick took off his sunglasses, exposing his eyeless face. Where there should have been eye sockets and eyes, was just smooth skin. There was no way Patrick could have ever had sight, as his body never even made room for eyes to develop and grow. This was the reason why he always wore the sunglasses. Most people assumed it was just due to him being blind. However, he wore them to also protect himself from the taunts and teasing from other kids for looking so different. Though he was young still, he had received his share of bullying already. Even his foster siblings, Peter, Colin and Clay, called him a freak when the older kids or the grownups weren't around to hear them.

"Stop it," Patrick repeated. He knew his sister was doing something she shouldn't be doing. He didn't know what it was and he wouldn't understand even if he did. In his mind, he had convinced himself that his twin sister was kind and could do no wrong. Although there were times he felt something was off and it had to do with his sister. Even though he sensed this, he only ever felt love and kindness for her. She wasn't bad to Patrick. She might be confused, but not bad.

Walking over to where Lily stood at the window sill,

he reached down and searched until he found her small hand. Standing together, shoulder to shoulder, hand in hand, he stood by her side. This love he had for his sister was the only thing he ever felt that was as real as life itself. Looking over at Patrick, Lily smiled as she returned to watch the ambulance arrive across the street.

Chapter 6
I Smell a Rat

O n a clear weekday morning, behind a large dumpster, three large rats were feasting on something bloody and gooey. With each nibble and bite there came crunching and slurping sounds, carried on the slight breeze along with the stench of decay. The three rats weren't overly large, but they had weird rippling and crawling flesh underneath the short, matted and dark fur that covered their misshapen bodies. One of the rats stopped eating to sniff the air, as if something was amiss. Something had caught its attention away from the much needed feast and the sustenance it would need to fuel its rapid growth. Its bloody snout sniffed at the air as it rose on its hind quarters, making its body long and lean. The rat hissed, catlike, and scurried away. A shuffling sound made the two other rats pause for a brief moment before following suit. The three rats scurried through a hole in a section of fence behind the Old Mill Restaurant and disappeared from sight, leaving behind their feast: the much larger, dead and rotting, body of their mother. Blood, pus and a yellow gooey substance oozed from the bite marks and missing flesh, but no flies buzzed around the dead thing. No flies would go near it.

Shuffling his feet, Burke kicked at an empty soda can,

sending it flying against the dumpster behind the Old Mill Restaurant, making a clattering sound. He dug out his Zippo from his pocket and lit a menthol cigarette. He knew these weren't good for him, but he also didn't know how else to keep from going completely crazy. He inhaled long on his smoke, which made him burst into a hacking, coughing fit that made his knees weak, his head spin and phlegm build in his mouth and throat.

Once he got his coughing under control, he spat and wiped the tears away from his eyes and took another drag. *I'll quit eventually*, he thought to himself. *Just not today.* The cell phone in his pocket made a bloop sound which indicated he had gotten a text.

I'm here was all it read.

The text was from Jin Hong. Jin was inside the Old Mill Restaurant waiting on Burke. He looked at his half-smoked cigarette before placing it between his lips to free his hands. He sent a little white lie in response.

I'm just up the street... be there soon.

Burke adjusted his large plastic framed glasses and blew out smoke. As soon as he finished exhaling, he winced at a sudden, horrible scent that assaulted his smoker's dulled sense of smell. Burke swatted at the air in hopes of alleviating the strength of the rotten odor. The stench was too much, even for his smoke damaged sinuses. He took a quick last drag of his cigarette and flicked it against the dumpster. Burke walked away as the stub of a cigarette rolled on the asphalt, still smoldering. A set of small, glowing yellow eyes peered at it from under the dumpster.

Moments later, the trio of misshapen rats returned once more to feast on the corpse of their mother. Years ago their mother had eaten from a strange plant in a cavern along the coast that had long since collapsed. The strange plant had gifted the mother rat with a long, though painful life, filled with illness and the occasional hunger that could not be fed. Its recent offspring had insatiable hunger and seemed to thrive.

Their first meal had been their father, their ravenous appetites being satiated while their mother watched. The strange rats mostly shunned by the collective murids would eventually feast on their inferior brothering. While hunting for food, a savage hunger overcame them and mother became prey. Mother became food. Such was the price to pay once this deep hunger took over.

"Detective Burke," Shelley exclaimed as he walked into the Old Mill Restaurant. "I can't say I'm happy to see you. It's never good when you're in town."

"It's great to see you too, Shelley," Burke replied with a sly grin. While on sick leave, he might not have been feeling his usual self, but he was still able to appreciate sarcasm. "I'm meeting a friend," Burke added as he saw Jin Hong raise his hand to get his attention. Jin sat at a cluttered table at the very back of the restaurant, which Burke thought was a good idea.

"Coffee?" Shelley asked.

"Sure," Burke replied. "And do you have any of your homemade pie?"

"Apple?" Shelley asked. "With ice-cream?"

"Bring one for my friend too," Burke replied as he made his way to the table where Jin sat.

Jin stood to greet Burke as he approached, holding out his hand for a handshake which Burke complied with.

"Nice to finally meet you in person," Jin said.

"Doesn't Skype count?" Burke asked as both men sat down.

Burke couldn't help but notice that the clutter on the table were some of the documents he had mailed to Hong, most of which he had been hesitant to send electronically, and chance leaving a digital trail. There were copies of autopsy reports, medical records, lab reports and a slew of pictures, many of which had garnered looks of disgust from Shelley when she accidentally saw more than she had wanted to.

"I have to admit when you first sent me the lab reports for my opinion, I assumed you guys were messing with me," Jin stated, wasting no time getting to the point. "The lab reports show a mutated strain of a fungus previously only found in the jungles of Peru."

"The vampire ants," Burke replied. "The ones you told me about."

Jin wasn't sure if Burke was testing him or if he really was confused.

"The zombie ants," Jin replied, correcting Burke. "Did you read the articles I sent you?"

"I did. But remember that I'm not a scientist."

"Well I am," Jin replied. "I wish I had those baggies you told me about. The ones the chamber maid said she threw out. I bet Danny was on to something."

"On to what?" Shelley asked as she brought over two heaping plates of apple pie, topped with ice-cream. "Does this have to do with the article in the Chronicler?"

"What article?" Burke inquired, who was already familiar with Oakwood Island's only surviving newspaper.

"The one about the dead animals they found out in the woods and more near town. Oh, they made a big deal out of it, just trying to scare people is what I think, going on about the five year anniversary of the killings. A cluster of dead animals too, near the old Stuart's house."

"You have a copy of that paper handy?" Burke asked.

"Sure do," Shelley replied. "I'll get you one. Be right back with your coffees."

"Thanks," Burke said, a sentiment which was echoed by Jin.

"I'll be honest," Burke continued as he turned his focus back to the man he had come to meet in person. "I read the article you sent me and I did a little digging of my own. Those ants you talk about sound like science fiction to me. Like something out of a bad Stephen King book." Burke picked up his fork and took a bite of pie.

"I assure you they're real," Jin replied with a frown as he was a big fan of King and his works. He set his fork down, took out a laptop and booted it up. He set it down on the table, on top of the papers and opened a folder of pictures. Jin turned the laptop so Burke could use it.

Burke ate pie as he scrolled through the images of weird ants with tiny mushroom like things that appeared to be growing on them. The old Burke would have used one of his favorite sarcastic lines, like how he had once seen a fifty foot ape climbing the Empire State Building too. He had often reminded people how easy it was, especially with today's technology to create fake news. The old Burke would have said this. Although he thought it, he didn't feel the need to say it this time, for fear of sounding ignorant. He knew Jin was a scientist and so he wouldn't bring anything to the table unless it was scientifically solid. Besides, he'd seen enough weird happenings on this island to make him doubt his sanity. He had learned to question things before discrediting the idea right off the bat.

"The thing I don't understand," Jin added, talking through a mouthful of pie. "I've never seen people get infected by this spore before. There have been other insects found to have fallen prey to such fungus." Jin swallowed his food and continued. "Certain species of cat-erpillars too, although our team has only been studying ants. While we take precautions, I've never seen anything remotely resembling any kind of infection on people. But this Maggie was riddled with this stuff. And I know you found syringes that had trace amounts, so that's the only thing that made sense to me. Although traces of the fungus on Danny's remains I assume got there as he was probably looking for samples or something when he died. And I don't believe your foolish theory that he was the one injecting Maggie with that crap. Danny wasn't Victor Frankenstein."

Burke paused at a picture as he swallowed a mouth-ful of pie. He pointed to the screen. "You're shitting me, right?" he asked.

"Nope," Jin replied, closing the laptop as he watched Shelley finally bring the coffees, the newspaper tucked under her arm.

"Sorry to take so long with the coffee, guys," Shelley said as she set the cups down and handed the newspaper to Burke.

"Front page," she added. "They even mention Peggy Martin's Pomeranian in the article. You know Peggy, right? She was Ryan's aunt. Anyway, it talks about her dog and how it was found half eaten. Bijou she called it, poor thing. Grady thinks the mayor and town council are trying to drum up tourism; the kind of people who go to Salem to see the place where they burned witches or to Maine to see Stephen King's house. Those types."

"Murders and gruesome deaths are a tourist attraction here?" Jin asked.

"Stranger things have happened," Burke added as he adjusted his glasses again on the rim of his nose.

"Grady thinks it's cool," Shelley added with a frown as

she walked away to serve another table.

"Grady's an idiot," Burke chuckled as he replied and began reading the article. Jin sipped his coffee and thought it best to not ask who this Grady fellow was and why they cared so much what Grady thought.

Chapter 7
Birds of a Feather

Jack Whitefeather sat cross-legged on the floor of the small, rustic cabin he called home, tucked neatly away in the thick forest on the center of the island he loved so much. His eyes were closed, his head bowed down with his long grey locks dangling freely, he was in deep meditation as smoke from the fragrant burning sage incense wafted in the air around him. His muffled chant, while barely audible, was the only indication that he wasn't actually asleep. The meditation was getting harder and harder to achieve. Calming his racing mind had never been an issue in the past but seeing visions that he didn't bring on himself was worrisome to the old man.

Connecting to his feathered friend seemed to be difficult now too, compared to before, as if the old crow was resisting him. This was something it had never done before which begged the question, why now, after all these years? Did it have something to do with the vision his crow had showed him when he wasn't in the process of reaching out to it? He still hadn't understood if what he'd seen was some sort of vision or if the spirit was real. Did he really see the spirit of his grandmother sitting next to him? If yes, was she here now? Was she in the room with him? Without looking through the bird's eyes, Jack couldn't see the spirits that roamed the island. And if she was here, what did she want? Why come to him now?

His low mumbled chant was labored as he struggled

to see through the crow while the bird flew high over the outskirts of town. He struggled to keep up with the bird; his visions were blurred and out of focus. The crow swooped down amidst homes, landing on a branch of a large oak tree overlooking a covered sandbox where a pair of children played.

Jack recognized the twins right away. He had heard of their birth years before and had spied on some of the staff at the hospital via his feathered friend. The doctors had thought Norah Jenkins was having twin girls, but they'd been wrong. This was due to an ultrasound error by a faulty machine at the hospital. It had been a surprise to everyone, even to Norah. She gave birth to a girl, yes but the other was a boy, a unique boy that was kept secret at first. But secrets are difficult to keep in small towns. Secrets like the boy's were even harder to keep private.

The twins lived at the orphanage at first, but Patrick's uniqueness made it difficult for him to fit in. The only friend he had was his twin sister who wasn't afraid, tormented or made fun of him. It wasn't his fault he was born without eyes but it was the reason he became famous. Born without eye sockets in his skull, Jack would later recall a newspaper article mentioning this. They had used scientific lingo Jack didn't understand but it was as if Patrick's brain didn't have the proper wiring for eyes and so his skull had not developed a place for his eyes to be. His forehead seemed normal, but the lack of eyebrows or eyes meant it sloped down to nose and cheeks. This was the reason he would soon find comfort hiding behind a large pair of dark sunglasses gifted to him by a kindhearted janitor at the orphanage. The very sunglasses he now wore while playing in the sandbox.

Norah Jenkins' twins lived with Scott and Miriam Cudmore; a couple who knew nothing of the history of the

Jenkins family. They knew nothing of a curse born sometime in the 1800's, which was the story Jack had been told by his late mother. Most of the Jenkins' descendants knew nothing of a curse; a curse that was kept hidden all too well. Those who Jack tried to tell called him crazy. The hospital and orphanage staff began to think he wasn't well with his questions about Norah Jenkins and her twins. Soon he learned that if he was to keep an eye on the twins or Norah, it was to be from a distance. That was the only way, as otherwise he might end up at the very place Norah now called home: the psychiatric wing of the Oakwood Island Hospital.

Jack watched through the crow from a branch in the oak tree as Lily held a large rock in both her hands and was in the process of flattening one of her new Barbie dolls. The dolls clothes were scattered on the ground next to the four-year-old girl as she smashed the doll over and over.

Patrick knelt in the sandbox, holding a plastic shovel and pail as he cocked his head, listening to the thudding of something he knew was coming from his sister. He didn't know the thumping sound was of the rock to the doll. Patrick dropped the shovel and started tugging at the crotch of his pants. He stood and cocked his head at different angles listening intently.

"Samantha? I have to pee," Patrick said.

The voices muffled and the vision blurred slightly as if in a haze, but Jack watched on. Next to Patrick, a shimmering glow appeared for a moment before coming into focus. Jack felt a wave of anxiety wash over him. While he was watching the scene unfold through the eyes of the crow, he felt his pulse rising and beads of sweat began to form soon after he realized what he was seeing. He saw what he now knew was the spirit of his grandmother, Sparrow

Whitefeather, standing at Patrick's side. His grandmother wore the same singed dress she had worn in her youth and in the only photo he had ever seen of her from that era. The spirit shone vividly as the vision Jack saw came into focus. Sparrow looked directly at the crow as if peering through it and at Jack himself. She placed her hand on the boy's head while peering back at him.

"Who's there?" Patrick whispered as he felt a strange presence next to him for a brief moment. The hair on his arms and on the back of his neck rose when he didn't get a response back.

Samantha, who had been sitting under the oak tree and out of sight for Jack, got up to tend to Patrick. She tucked her book under her arm and reached for the boy's hand as the spirit stood stock still next to the boy.

"Come," Samantha said as she placed her hand in the blind boy's now outstretched hand. "You too, Lily."

"But I don't gotta pee," Lily answered, frowning as she gave the battered Barbie doll one last hard smash with the rock.

"I can't leave you out here alone and you know that, little lady. Now put down that rock like I told you to, before you hurt yourself and come," Samantha added.

Sparrow Whitefeather's glow intensified until it flashed from a bright silver light into a pure white platinum, waking Jack from his trance to find himself clammy with perspiration.

Jack wondered if the crow somehow was called to the house while Jack watched through it. Did it somehow know this would happen? Or did the spirit of his grandmother come there because he was watching? Why did she touch the boy? What was she trying to tell him?

Did this have anything to do with Ben Augustine's accident? That had to have been caused by one of the twins.

Jack still wasn't sure which one bore the curse. From what he knew, only one child would bear it at a time. He knew his grandmother knew about the curse. He had no reason to doubt the stories his mother told him, not after everything he had seen. Surely his grandmother didn't want him to kill the twins, he briefly wondered. Doing that would be pointless while Norah still lived.

Jack had believed that she would be the end of the curse after being confined and having lost her mind. How she had managed to have twins while locked away in a psychiatric ward of a hospital was still a mystery. But Jack was still adamant in his belief that killing the twins would just mean somehow the curse would continue through Norah. The only other living descendants of the Jenkins family were of such distant relation that Jack didn't fear them being pulled into this. Somehow she would have another set of twins. He couldn't understand how but he felt this to be true. And sneaking into the hospital to kill Norah wouldn't help little Patrick and Lily.

Wiping the sweat off his forehead with the sleeve of his faded red shirt, Jack took a tin from his kitchen and went outside to sit on his handmade chair made of tree branches. There he cracked open the tin, pulled out a joint and lit it in hopes of it helping to steady his nerves. It's a spirit, he thought to himself, but why? He had seen many restless spirits on Oakwood Island, but never of his own ancestors. The spirits clung to this island. The spirits he saw with the help of the crow were confused, troubled, lost and sometimes angry. Sparrow Whitefeather was none of those things. At least she wasn't until now, thought Jack as he inhaled deeply from his joint, closed his eyes and waited for the herbal medicine to take effect.

Perhaps he needed help, he thought. Maybe he could get help to figure this out. Jack had his own beliefs when it came to spirits. Unlike most people, he had seen them and knew they were real. But this felt like it was beyond his abilities. He knew he had to do something about it. *I'll make a call to get help*, he thought, as he took another drag from his joint. It was worth a try.

Chapter 8
Conceived from Love, Born in Hate
Year: 1899

The drought that had held Oakwood Island in its oppressive grasp was still being felt in 1899. Though not as bad as the year before, most were hopeful that the crops would be better this season. Harvest had been thin in the fall and had produced very little for the families that had settled in the area and had built farms for cattle, livestock and vegetable crops. The fishermen from the mainland were having a lot more luck than the island families that were dependent on their crops and livestock. Some had returned to the mainland, where there was work at least in the fisheries and on the fishing boats. Work meant money to be able to buy food from the ones that had a bit extra to go around. Life on the island was not easy, but those who stayed worked hard to make sure they would have enough to survive, at the very least.

Henri Masterson no longer cared for farming. He no longer had the patience to tend to it, to watch things grow. He also did not want to spend all his days and nights on a cold and wet fishing boat, surrounded with loud and mostly drunk fishermen, the saltwater beating his face and patience. Instead, he hunted and trapped for meat. He would cut wood for lumber and firewood when he wasn't hunting, often trading with neighboring families for goods or services they needed, all while Sparrow cared for the children.

Sparrow Whitefeather spent most of her time helping Henri care for the one year old twins. Henri both loved and hated his children. He wanted to love them with all his heart, like his late wife would have wanted, but he found himself often glaring at them, his heart filled with a hate he could not control. He spent days and weeks in his mind, his thoughts filled with blaming them for his wife's death, even though she had not died due to giving birth. His wife had bled to death after being cut by Bessie.

Sparrow recognized his conflicted thoughts, and picked up on the ill feelings towards the children. She tried to talk to Henri, to bring some sense to him in regards to his wife's death and who had caused it. She speculated that Bessie wanted the child and cared not if the mother had lived. So she had cut her, making the baby come faster in order to take it and run before Henri returned with the water. All that Bessie had wanted was to get to her sacrificial site and kill the baby as planned, to offer it to whatever devil she had made a deal with.

Sparrow had told Henri that Bessie had been crazy, but she wondered to herself if perhaps there was more to it. Since Sparrow stopped the murder of an innocent child in what looked like some sort of ritual, strange things had started happening. Things Sparrow couldn't understand nor explain with logic, which lead her to doubt her own sanity at times. This was often due to fatigue though, she told herself. She knew several mothers that often became but shadows of the bright young women they had once been as soon as they delivered a baby. And even though she had not carried them in her body, and given birth to them, taking care of two babies surely had taken its toll on Sparrow, and she concluded that perhaps that was all it was.

As tired as she may have become over the last twelve

full moons, she saw how Henri looked at the children sometimes and didn't want to leave them in his care. She feared he would hurt them if she did. Now pregnant herself, she felt an even greater need to protect the children. Her husband didn't understand when she told him that she had to protect the twins. He couldn't grasp how a father could wish harm on his own children. Sparrow hadn't yet told her husband that she herself was now with child. She couldn't as then she knew with certainty he wouldn't let her care for the Masterson twins. She had to come up with a plan and soon. She loved the baby twin boy and girl too much to let any harm come their way.

Sparrow Whitefeather had taken to calling the little twin girl Nakuset, which meant Sunshine. She called her this because of the brightness of her spirit. She seemed to glow with life and so Nakuset/Sunshine suited her fine. As she bathed Nakuset, her twin brother lay naked on the bed, kicking and cooing as he finished drying from his bath. She called him Gaqtugwawig, or Gaqtu for short, which meant Thunder. This name she chose for the way he screamed and carried on when he was upset. She had decided to name them as Henri had never named his children. He shunned the subject every time Sparrow brought it up by leaving the cabin and disappearing for hours on end. When Sparrow first tried to name the girl Martha after their late mother, Henri grew so angry that he threw a chair across the kitchen and it broke several dishes on the countertop. His outburst had frightened her and the babies. Moments later, he had left them alone in the cabin, not returning for several days. Eventually, she decided to give the baby girl the name that meant Sunshine instead of naming her after Martha.

The one-year-old twins, as much as she loved and cared for them as best she could, had become her burden. She couldn't leave them with Henri for long anymore. In the beginning, she could leave them for a few days and he would look after them, though he did so with no love, no care in his heart. The last time she had done so, she had found them alone in the cabin when she returned. Henri had gone hunting and left the children, hungry and cold. She decided from that day forward that he could not be trusted with them for much more than a few hours at a time. She made it a point from that day to care for the babies daily.

Sparrow frowned, lost in her thoughts about Henri's lack of care, as she placed the little girl on the bed, next to her twin brother. She turned her attention to the pot-bellied wood stove that warmed the cabin so the children would be comfortable. She placed a new log of wood to the fire, and added more water from a wood pail to a large pot on the stove. Turning her attention to the cooing children, Sparrow smiled. Placing a hand on her small baby bump, she felt the love growing from inside her as much as she loved the twins she had felt forced to care for at first. She wanted to take them with her when she left, unsure when Henri would return from hunting, but her husband wouldn't understand. She feared for the babies but was unsure how to save them from the life they had been born into.

She wiped them a bit with a cloth, drying off the bathwater, and dressed them in their light cotton sleeping gowns. She watched them as they both yawned and began to slip off into slumber; the warmth of the stove helping them to sleep. Thunder had rumbled prior to his bath, screaming and crying, while at the same time, Sunshine had lay quietly sucking her thumb as she often did during his rants. It was as if her brother's cries soothed her. The twins slipped off to sleep in unison.

Sparrow heard what she thought was her water boiling on the old wood stove but when she turned her attention to it, she saw the water was still, without a hint of steam yet, let alone boiling. The noise repeated itself, and seemed to come from outside. It had been a beautiful day when last she looked, but now she heard what had to be strong winds battering the cabin. Had the winds grown stronger? *Is there some sort of storm brewing*, thought Sparrow as she went to the door to see.

Opening the door, she spotted dark clouds in the sky blocking out the sunshine she had seen not long ago. In the far off distance, she saw a dark figure lurking in the shadows near the brush that surrounded the cabin's yard. She turned to check on the children and saw them peacefully sleeping on the bed. When Sparrow turned her attention outside again, the figure was no longer in the brush but standing twenty feet from the cabin. It stood in a wide pentagram made of flames that were as high as the figure's waist. The flickering flames cast much light but somehow, the figure remained draped in shadows. It had to be Bessie thought Sparrow. But how was she doing this? It had to be dark magic of some sort. The figure raised its arms, palms up and the flames grew taller.

"What do you want from us? Leave!" Sparrow cried out, tears welling up in her eyes. She couldn't believe her eyes. She had been so sure Bessie had died that day just over a year ago.

"Go away with your dark magic! We want none of it here! You are not welcome!"

Sparrow looked back at the children who still seemed to sleep peacefully. Sunshine sucked her thumb while

Thunder lay sleeping next to her.

Sparrow picked up one of Henri's smaller axes that sat near the door and charged at the figure in the flaming pentagram at full speed. She raised the axe overhead as she ran, hoping to scare off the figure, but it stood there, arms stretched overhead, flames growing high. Reaching the flames, she ran through them and brought the axe down on the figure. Down went the axe, through thin air, the figure gone, the flames and the pentagram also gone. The axe hit the dirt with a thud and sent a cloud of dust around the sharp slit mark it left in the ground. Picking it up in a swift movement, she clutched it as if waiting to be attacked. She looked around perplexed at what had just happened. As her breathing slowed, she felt confusion and fear set in. Had she imagined her? The dark figure whom she assumed was Bessie? Was it her spirit? Confused, she stood in front of the cabin a few moments until the sound of crackling coming from behind her made fear swell up inside her. Sparrow spun around to see the entire cabin engulfed in flames.

"Nooooooo..." she screamed, her legs feeling weak as she dropped to her knees, the axe thudding onto the ground before her. "No!"

"Sparrow!" she heard someone shout. "Sparrow... what's wrong?"

Sparrow buried her face in her hands and wept hard. She felt strong hands grasp her shoulders and shake her. Sparrow looked up at the bearded man who had driven the cart on the night the twins were born.

"Sparrow, is it the children?" the bearded man demanded. "Tell me!"

Sparrow looked at the bearded man in stunned silence as she saw the blue sky overhead.

"Fire..." she began, but stopped. Glancing past the man

she saw the cabin, perfectly fine and not a sign of any fire damage.

"Have I gone mad?" Sparrow asked the large, bearded man, tears streaming down her cheeks.

"What?" the bearded man asked. "Sparrow, where are the twins?"

Sparrow, still kneeling on the ground, pointed towards the cabin.

The large bearded man turned and ran to the open door expecting to find something horrible. Sparrow had been shrieking after all. Instead he found the twins, lying on their bed; the boy fast asleep but the girl sucking her thumb. She popped it out of her mouth and began cooing and smiling up at the man as he smiled back at her.

Henri sat at the wooden table in his home with a near empty plate before him. He watched with disdain as the twins played in a makeshift play area Sparrow had fashioned using boards in a corner of the cabin. The boy had taken to crawling early and now was walking with unsteady steps at thirteen months. The girl seemed content to sit, often just staring off into the distance when she wasn't her usually bright cheerful self. Sparrow had gone to fetch water, wash clothes and clean the cast iron skillet. She had insisted that Henri keep an eye on his children. Henri could tell that she had been hesitant to do so. He had been trying to keep his anger under control over the past week, or at the very least hidden from Sparrow. He did not want her to think that he was not able to father his own children. When she insisted that he look after them, he knew he had succeeded. Otherwise, she would never have left him with them alone.

She had instructed Henri to simply keep an eye on the twins while she did her chores. She wouldn't be too long. She explained to Henri how Thunder had gotten out of the makeshift pen a few times already, and Sparrow was afraid he'd burn himself on the stove if he got out unattended. Henri had grumbled his agreement to tend to them while Sparrow did chores. As he ate his meal, he watched them with disdain. Henri wasn't done blaming the twins for their mother's death. He couldn't stand to look at them. He hated them still.

Henri ate the last of his potato, as he poked his knife at the last morsel of boiled rabbit on his plate. He heard the twins cooing but couldn't bear to look at them, instead focusing on the meat before him. He ate the last of the rabbit while wishing his wife still lived. He missed her greatly. She had always made him happy, even in difficult times. But he had lost her, and it was their fault.

Henri heard a rustling noise coming from the pen area, but he couldn't bring himself to look. He hated those children. He felt as if his blood boiled, his face flushed, and his stomach knotted as he listened to the twins coo. He didn't think he had the patience to watch them grow after they took his Martha. He listened to them shuffle about but refused to look. He refused that is, until he heard one the children speak what sounded like a word.

"Mama," he heard the tiny voice say as a tear ran down his cheek as he thought of his Martha. She had wanted children, many children. He knew because she had told him often enough. Now her children would grow up never knowing who their mother was. He wiped away his tears as he turned to see the children but saw they were no longer in the pen. He heard a squeal of happiness coming from one of the twins. On the bed was a familiar looking fabric. Both twins sat on the bed, on his late wife's blood-covered dress. The girl child smiled and laughed while the boy spoke.

"Mmmm... mamma!"

Sitting atop the blood smeared dress, the twins toyed with the fabric, getting blood on their hands as they smiled. They smiled and laughed. The boy child stuffed a bloody hand in his mouth, took it out and spoke.

"Momma!" he said with a scowl as his twin sister laughed.

Rage fueled Henri as he rose from the table, sending the chair he sat on tumbling backwards. It clattered and struck the wall behind him. He walked to the door of the cabin with the intention of going outside but stopped at the door.

"MOMMA!!" he heard coming from behind him.

Looking down to his left, Henri picked up his heaviest axe, marched to the bed and without hesitation began hacking at the twins. Blood spattered his face as he brought the axe down on the small bodies again and again, destroying the bed as well in the process. The maddening rage that had fueled the onslaught subsided as his head spun and he staggered, taking a step backwards. He looked at the carnage before him; the small bodies completely hacked to pieces and gore splatter covering the dress, the bed and walls. Bewildered, Henri dropped the axe and looked at his trembling blood covered hands. What had he done? How could he explain this to Sparrow? He remembered his dead wife and her love of children. He had killed their children, her babies. Looking back up at the bloodied, decimated bodies of the two infant children, he knew what he had to do.

Sparrow saw the cabin door was open as she approached and that worried her. *Has Henri left the twins alone again*, she wondered? She carried a skillet in one hand and a bucket containing freshly washed garments in the other. She wanted to run but was afraid of what she might find when she got there. Henri had seemed better recently, less angry. The sight of the open cabin door worried her. She set the bucket down before stepping inside but kept hold of the cast iron skillet. She stopped and stood in the doorway. The skillet fell from her hand, hitting the wooden floor with a clang. Sparrow's scream echoed in every corner of the small cabin.

Henri's lifeless body dangled from a rope tied to a rafter, a chair toppled over at his feet. Sparrow hesitated, but then stepped into the cabin, her thoughts returning to the babies. When she saw the wood bed and straw mattress in the corner had been chopped to pieces, most likely with the axe that lay on the floor next to it, she gasped. Just as soon as panic began to well up in her abdomen, it was squashed when she saw Wallace, the large bearded man who had driven the cart to fetch her on the night the twins were born. Standing next to the children's pen, he held Thunder in his arms, his face tear-stained as the little boy grabbed at the big man's beard. Sunshine stood by the edge of the pen holding herself up, smiling at the large bearded man.

The children were fine after all, but Henri was dead and by his own hand. As much as she loved the children she had cared for, she knew this was the end of her journey with them. Turning back towards the cabin's door, she ran out, ignoring the tears that ran down her face. She knew she had to protect her own baby that grew bigger every day in her belly. She could not let what she now believed was a curse on these babies affect her own unborn child. Sparrow wondered if something was wrong with the children. Were they possessed by an evil that she could not see? They had been exposed to Bessie at birth and Sunshine had been used in a ritual that Bessie had tried to do on the night the girl twin was born. She had no clear idea of what this curse was, but she knew this was something she could never tell anyone if she was to be rid of the burden of caring for someone else's children while expecting her own. With a man like Wallace and his family to care for them, they would be better off, so Sparrow ran.

Wallace and his eldest son had already constructed a makeshift bed for the twins. They would sleep in the same bedroom as Wallace and his wife Hester. The Masterson twins needed caring for and there was no one else to do it. That decision would not come without their share of worries.

Wallace had explained to his wife that Sparrow had run away after seeing the lifeless body of Henri dangling from a rope. She hadn't said a word to Wallace when she saw he had the children in his care. She had just bolted outside and had been seen by Hester as she ran away from the cabin where Henri had taken his life.

Hester and Wallace discussed at great lengths the situation before they agreed to take in the children and care for them, as there was nobody else for miles, and even if they did go look for help for the twins, they knew they would be likely locked away in an orphanage somewhere. This was not something the loving couple could let happen.

Later that night in their home, in the warm glow of lanterns, their own children already sleeping away the tiredness of chores, the couple conversed.

"I'm not sure I can raise these children with names like Thunder and Sunshine," Hester said. "I know Sparrow said Henri never wanted to name the children, but Wallace, if they're to be ours now," she said, trailing off as she raised the little smiling girl into the air. Hester smiled wide at her, making the child giddy with laughter.

"Jenkins children need names," Wallace said to the boy he cradled on his lap. "We will call you Liam." He had heard the name on the wharf. One of the boat captains had been named Liam and he thought it suited the boy.

"Fannie," Hester added with a smile. "We will call you Fannie," she said to the little girl as she dressed her in warm clothes that used to belong to their own daughter when she had been little.

"Welcome to the Jenkins family," Hester said. She shed a single tear of happiness. Hester had wanted more children in recent years, but it hadn't looked like it would happen. With two growing children of their own, she had not been able to bear any more. The twins had to be a gift from God, she thought. Finally, her prayers had been answered. She would think that way for a while still.

It would take some time for the evil embedded in the little girl to show itself again. She would love the children fiercely even when it finally did.

Chapter 9
Grady
Early July

Grady stood behind the Old Mill Restaurant, gripping two smelly trash bags in his hands. The dumpster lid was propped open with a rotting piece of wood and he stared at it, then at the bag in his hand. Could he throw it into the dumpster from where he stood? The last time he tried that, it had hit the side of the dumpster and burst open, strewing trash all over the asphalt. All while Shelley had been watching him through her small office window. No matter how much he insisted he had seen a rat near the dumpster, Shelley angrily insisted he clean his mess, which Grady did reluctantly while cursing his own stupidity the entire time.

Grady needed this job. He hadn't needed it, that is, until he'd crashed his father's car while doing donuts in the church parking lot. He needed this job to pay for the damages to the car and to replace the large metal donation bin he had crashed the car into. The bin was used to drop off used clothing and articles by community members trying to help out their fellow islanders. It had been smashed open, spreading its contents all over the asphalt. Clothing, lamps, and dishes had been sprawled out everywhere. The metal box had been bent out of shape, the door detached, and the paint scratched. There had been no way to repair it and so it needed to be replaced. This was why he needed this job, he remembered, as he arched his arm back, ready to throw the bag. The memories of his luck with spreading things all over parking lots and the stench of the garbage bag were the deciding factors against the idea.

"Third time's the charm, my posterior," he muttered, thinking himself clever. He walked to the dumpster while dragging his feet. He tossed a bag into the dumpster and winced at the smell as he did. He gagged at the rancid stench as it washed over him.

"What's in that?" he muttered to himself as he cleverly tossed the second bag into the dumpster in a way that it struck the wood in the process, knocking it into the dumpster and slamming the lid shut in one fell swoop. Pinching his nostrils shut with his fingers, he looked around to see if anyone had seen his really cool toss and lid closing trick. Of course, nobody was around, he thought as he wished someone had seen him. He glanced at the window of Shelley's office to see if she was watching and felt disappointed when she wasn't.

A scuffling sound behind him caught Grady's attention. He turned his focus back to the dumpster. On top of the now closed lid sat the biggest rat he had ever seen. Spooked, he took a single step back as the rat raised itself on its hind legs and hissed at him like a cat. Before he could react, the rat's neck jutted forward and with its mouth open it sprayed the teen's face with a hot, sticky, and rancid liquid.

"Fuck!" Grady exclaimed as he stumbled backwards a few steps before falling on his ass. He couldn't see anything at first, the sticky substance blinding him. He wiped at his eyes with the sleeve of his shirt trying to see. He panicked, thinking the rat was going to attack him. Struggling to see, he scurried away from the dumpster backwards. His vision began to clear, specks of light pricking the darkness, but everything was blurry; he couldn't see the rat anywhere. His eyes began to burn as he struggled to his feet. With one hand outstretched and the other wiping at his eyes, he stumbled to the back door of the restaurant. He made his way to the back room, found the eye wash station near the first aid kit and felt at it blindly, trying to understand how to use it.

Shelley, hearing Grady stumble about came to check on him. She saw him feeling around the eye wash station with his eyes closed and slime on his face. She pulled the cap off the eye wash station and helped Grady place his face on it.

"Keep your eyes open," Shelley stated firmly at Grady while watching him struggle to flush his eyes. "What is that stuff?" she blurted, thinking this was so typical of Grady to do something stupid like this.

Meanwhile, Grady uttered a series of curse words while he struggled to keep his eyes open to flush them out. The burning sensation still raged inside his lids, but it seemed to dissipate with each flush of the cool eye wash liquid.

Once his eyes were cleaned and the slime seemed to be all gone, they went to the parking lot and got in Shelley's car. On the drive to the ER, Grady eventually told her the tale of the large rat and how it had spit the slime all over him. Shelley assumed that Grady was lying, trying to cover up something stupid he had done. After all, it wouldn't be the first time he had done that. Besides, who ever heard of a giant rat that spit at you? Grady was definitely lying.

Later that night, with help from his mother, Grady had applied more eye drops prescribed that afternoon by Doctor Kingsley at the ER. His eyes stung still but it was mild now. The redness around his eyes hadn't gone away. It actually had gotten worse with the constant rubbing. His vision had been fine most of the day; although he had spent most of his time laying in the dark with his eyes closed, listening to music from his cell phone, trying to alleviate the occasional itching without scratching.

He now stood before the mirror in the bathroom, examining the redness around his eyes. Grady tried to blink away the blurred vision and it worked at first. His vision cleared and he saw the redness of the contour of his eyes clearly. His eyes became itchy as his vision blurred again.

His doctor had suggested he could use regular eye drops in between his medication if he needed it as it would help with the itching. Grady put in several drops, hoping for relief.

Sleep wouldn't come easy to him that night, but it came nonetheless. In a fitful dream, Grady was standing behind the Old Mill Restaurant again, but this time the rat was as big as a horse. It gave chase and eventually caught him, clawing his eyes out of his head as he tried to fight it off.

When he woke, the bed was damp with perspiration and his eyes felt like they were on fire. Grady clumsily grabbed his eye drops off his nightstand, stumbled to the bathroom and sat on the toilet. He leaned back, tilting his head and struggled to get drops into his eyes. Annoyed and in pain, he managed to get relief by emptying half the small bottle in the process, most of it running down his face. With his eyes closed, the cooling sensation of the drops took over, giving him a feeling of relief at last. Still seated, he began urinating while thinking he should have thrown the damn bags like he had wanted to in the first place.

Chapter 10
Old Friends

On the mainland, in the kitchen of a small house on a Mi'kmaq reserve sat three men.

"Is it true?" Ben Augustine asked from the wheelchair he now felt trapped in. "Is it true that you can speak to crows?" Ben had spent time working on Oakwood Island and had heard the rumors about the man that was seated at the table across from him in Chief Paul "Big Bear" Augustine's home.

Jack ignored the question and instead asked one of his own.

"Is it true you might never walk again?"

Jack had heard that Ben Augustine's accident had happened across from Scott Cudmore's house, the foster home where the twins now lived. This was something he felt was not a simple coincidence, but he couldn't tell this to Ben. At least not directly.

"Well, my legs started tingling two days ago, but it stopped again," Ben replied. "The doctor said that was a good sign, but it's too early to know for sure." Ben's eyes cast downwards, and his gaze drifted onto the tabletop. Deep in thought, he closed his eyes as he let out a soft sigh. It had been a very traumatizing ordeal, and he was still trying to understand the full scope of his injuries himself, let alone trying to explain it to someone else. He had hoped that Jack's visit to the reserve would provide him with a distraction. He was a bit disappointed that the conversation turned towards him, and he tried to hide this by not looking Jack in the eyes.

Seated at the kitchen table opposite Jack was a much older man known to him, as well as many others, as Big Bear, a man whose face showed his age. Sunken cheeks below large cheekbones, deep wrinkles and long white hair made him look old and wise. With age came wisdom and knowledge and this was why Jack had decided to travel to the mainland to seek his help. Jack ignored what the younger people of the reserve said about Big Bear. Most everyone under thirty said Big Bear was crazy simply because of the stories he recounted from his own childhood that had sounded improbable and far-fetched. Jack knew what that was like, because some Oakwood Island residents said the same about him. Here on the mainland, his feathered friend never followed. The crow would often fly over the ferry as Jack left the island, but it never followed any further. The crow always circled back to the island to await his return. This helped Jack avoid spreading those rumors about himself on the mainland more than they already had.

As he sat with the man that his friends had suggested he speak to, he wondered if the old man would help him. Seeing as his own grandson, Ben Augustine had already commented about Jack's ability to "speak" with crows. He knew his friends on the reserve meant well when they had suggested maybe Big Bear could help, as he too had had experiences with spirits trapped on this plane in his own lifetime, a long time ago. Jack wondered though if he could trust him, knowing that the rumors about his own abilities had already reached the old man.

Big Bear wasn't the Chief on the reserve anymore. He had long ago been replaced when his health had become frail. He had been replaced by a much younger man who didn't speak of spirits and great evils. The old ways were forgotten by many of the younger residents of the reserve, but some elders were convinced Big Bear wasn't lost in his own mind like so many believed. They were confident that if anyone could help Jack, it was him. The pair seemed to be cut from the same cloth, one of his friends had expressed.

While on Oakwood Island, a few of them had seen Jack interact with the crow and assumed it was a pet of sorts. Many of his friends from the mainland had heard tales of how Jack often knew things he shouldn't or couldn't possibly know. It was as if he had a special connection to the island and its people. There was something strange about Jack even if he never spoke about it. That was, he had never spoken about it until now. When he spoke of a spirit coming to him, it didn't take long for them to send the Crow Whisperer to the Reserve's own man who claimed he spoke to lost and trapped spirits.

Big Bear wasn't a very talkative man. He said only what needed to be said, when he felt the other was listening to what he had to say. When Jack arrived on Big Bear's stoop the previous night with stories of spirits, Big Bear knew why they had sent Jack to him. He had listened carefully to the stories of cursed twins and restless spirits residing on Oakwood Island. He had listened to Jack explain how he saw the spirits through his link to a special crow and how he had done so since his childhood. Jack had explained how he was always the one to do this. He explained how until now, the crow had never showed him a spirit without him initiating it. His feathered friend had never come to him and showed him a spirit like it had when his grandmother had come to him. Big Bear offered to help him in the only way he knew how, by having a traditional sacred pipe ceremony in order to communicate with the spirits, to make Jack's need of clarification known and to receive guidance and answers from the ancestors. Ben, a pipe carrier from birth, would guide the sacred ceremony, as he was the only one with this calling and gift in the area.

When night fell, the trio gathered in the backyard of Big Bear's home, under the hundreds of stars that speckled the sky.

"The sky is welcoming us, watching us with its many eyes in anticipation." Big Bear looked upwards and smiled broadly as he pointed towards the heavens. "Come, let us prepare."

He and Jack walked over to the far end of the property, where the lawn ended a few feet away from the river that passed through the land. A small fire was already burning in the fire pit near Ben's wheelchair. Ben sat with a thick wool blanket covering his legs. Resting on his lap was the oblong leather carrying case, golden yellow with dark brown and red beading designs adorning it. Ben smiled as Jack and Big Bear sat on the dusty straw mats that had been used for several generations in this sacred gathering spot.

"Let us begin by cleansing ourselves, brothers." The old man took out a small brown satchel, pulled apart the strings that kept it tied together and removed sage from the bag. He placed the dried sage leaves in a good-sized abalone shell, which served as a bowl. Once he lit the sage with the flame of the fire pit, he smudged himself with the swirling smoke and passed the shell over to Jack, who took his time to smudge himself before passing it to Ben, who did the same.

Ben removed the pipe from the yellow carrying case

and smudged it before repeating the cleansing all over the long instrument, from the bowl to the stem. He loaded the pipe in four parts, offering a pinch of tobacco to each of the four directions, as he addressed the spirits in each and asked them to hear their prayers tonight. Once the circle of offerings to the four directions was complete, he returned his wheelchair to its initial position facing the fire with the help of his grandfather. He brought the pipe up over his head, thanking the Creator for hearing their prayers and expressing gratitude for the answers to their questions and prayers. An owl hooted nearby. The three men looked at each other, their eyes reflecting the warm glow of the fire, as they acknowledged their presence was now made up of more than three mere mortals. The flames grew larger for a few seconds, yet no wind was felt.

When the flames died down and the fire returned to its previous crackle, Ben leaned over and placed the tip of a sweet grass braid in the flames. Once ignited, he blew on it a few times until only a red glow remained. He brought the burning braid to the bowl of the pipe and lit the tobacco as he inhaled a few times in the stem of the sacred pipe. As he did so, he sent his prayers up towards the skies, the smoke carrying them up to the spirits who would hear them as they were carried with the sacred smoke. Once completed, he smudged himself with the smoke four times, turning the stem clockwise between each to honor the four directions once more. Once completed, he passed the pipe over to Jack who was seated on the ground to his left.

Jack repeated the ceremonial process, as it had been taught to him as a young boy so very long ago. He had only ever taken part in a pipe ceremony as a young man, when he had questioned his life direction. As he began sending his prayers and questions to the elder spirits, he had an idea but was unsure if he should attempt it or not. Inhaling and sending another gust of smoke to the heavens above, he heard the owl hoot once more and in the distance a howling made its way to his ears. He took this as a confirmation from the elder spirits that they wanted him to proceed in order to get the answers he sought. He closed his eyes as the smoke swirled above him and called upon his feathered friend who had remained on Oakwood Island. Never before had he been able to communicate with the crow while off the island, but he felt the urge to try and he knew that by doing so, he could possibly find answers.

Still seated, eyes closed, he felt himself become very light, a floating sensation coming over him. All around him was darkness, but swirls of smoke appeared, engulfing him completely, transporting him somewhere else. Once the smoke cleared, he found himself sitting in a mist covered field, his grandmother sitting directly in front of him. Her face old, wrinkled, as it had been in her final years, how he remembered her well. She looked at him with love in her eyes, a smile that echoed her feelings for him. She held both her hands to her chest, dark and leather-like, then she held them out to him in a slow gesture. He noticed she wore the light brown dress, the one with the singe mark on the chest. The one she had worn in her younger years. Opening his mouth, he realized he could not speak. She sat quietly, looking at him with love in her eyes. Yet with all the love she was sending him, Jack felt an uneasiness overcome him. He could feel something was wrong in this field where the tall grasses hid them from their surroundings. He felt something lurking all around them, almost like an evil presence was watching, waiting to pounce on them both. Looking around, he only saw the tall grass filled with dew as the mist became thicker, cloud-like almost. In an instant, it passed over his grandmother's face and she was gone.

In her place sat a woman Jack knew well named Edwina Quartley, dressed in her mail carrier uniform. She too sat unwavering, as silent as Sparrow had been. Jack's pulse spiked and he felt his mouth go dry. Trying to move, he found himself unable to. Confused, he tried to speak but could not. The air around him felt heavier, the mist seemed to weigh on him with dread. To his right he noticed the tall grass moving, a dark shadow in the corner of his eye seemed to jump behind him. When he returned his gaze to Edwina, he gasped as he saw her eyes spilling blood, running down her face and cheeks and on the front of her uniform where it dripped in a continual flow.

The mist again and in a flash appeared Ben Augustine, eyes completely black, dark smoke swirled out of his ears, nose and opened mouth. Before Jack could even begin to comprehend what he was seeing, Ben was replaced with old man Ketchum. Mr. Ketchum smiled at Jack, which made him apprehensive, but as he watched the old man open his smiling mouth wide, hundreds of large black flies flew out and headed in all directions in a buzzing cloud. They swirled around Jack's head, swarming and recollecting until they shot back towards Mr. Ketchum, covering his face completely. Only once they were gone, Officer Ryan McGregor sat in front of Jack. Blood flowed from gashes and wounds; his face was partially missing. The flesh looked ragged as if it had been torn off. Jack tried to scream, to move, but it was no use. He was trapped here, forced to watch the many faces that were coming to him, one by one.

Officer Ryan pulled on a flap of loose skin that dangled on his cheek and as he pulled harder Jack could see another cheek, smooth and white under the bloody one. Ryan tugged hard until his whole face slid off. Jack blinked, stunned by what he was witnessing. The wind around him grew stronger, the tall grass whipped in every direction, hitting his face. Before him now sat Maggie, in her wait-ress uniform like Jack remembered her. She was looking to her left, searching the grass for something, perhaps the dark shadow Jack thought he had seen mere moments before. As she turned her stare to face Jack, only half of her face remained. He noticed her entire left side; both face and body looked like it had been crushed. The only thing that remained was a bloody mess.

Jack's panic continued to rise. He blinked fast only to see that Maggie was no longer in front of him, but now Norah Jenkins took her place. Her eyes blood red, she smiled to expose pointy teeth, covered in blood as pus dripped in heavy globs down her chin. Mrs. Ketchum soon replaced Norah, her dead corpse rotting, yet alive, mag-gots and worms wriggling in and out of her nose and ears. When she opened her mouth to talk, several came slid-ing out instead of words escaping her. Jack could hear his heartbeat thumping in his ears, beating hard in his chest. Behind the dead woman, he sensed the evil again; a dark shadow slithered in the small crevices in between the blades of grass.

He thought he could hear panting, some kind of an ani-mal nearby, perhaps, waiting to pounce on him. Before he could try to move again, Mrs. Ketchum was gone. In her place sat a very young, small girl. He knew the young girl was Lily. She sat up straight, smiling up at him, her cute little face as normal as he remembered. He began to calm down, until her smile began to turn into a grin, her little lips curling up at the edges into a sly smile, her brow fur-rowing. He looked at her, unsure what to think. The wind turned violent, whipping the grass all around, sending his hat flying off his head and out into the field beyond, making him close his eyes from fear. When he reopened them, there sat Sparrow, his loving grandmother, just as before, quiet and unwavering. Her calm demeanor brought peace to him once more. She still held her hands to her chest.

Finally able to move, he reached up both his hands, looked at her and spoke in a soft tone.

"Nukumi..." he uttered.

Just as his hands reached hers, two large bloody claws protruded from her chest and through her body. The evil that had lurked in the shadows had snuck up behind her. Jack saw a hairy scalp with dog-like ears and glowing red eyes begin to appear from behind Sparrow, just as all went black.

Jack Whitefeather woke up from what felt like a long sleep, yet he was still sitting in the same position on the straw mat in the backyard. He had no idea how long he had been sitting there, but he knew it had been many hours, since he could see that the sun would soon rise. Dawn's arrival had hidden the stars above, the elder spirits long gone, as well as Ben and his wheelchair, which were nowhere to be seen. Big Bear now lay on his side on his mat, his hands tucked in to keep himself warm. Facing the dying embers of the fire from the night before, his snores were long and deep.

As Jack drifted off to sleep again, he dreamt of Edwina Quartley. A woman he knew but couldn't fathom how she was tied to this. The rest of the ones he had seen in his mind's eye he knew were tied to this, but not Edwina. When he awoke again in the morning, the bright July sun shone on his face through the branches of the willow trees near the river. Getting up, he found his body was sore and weak. He was not accustomed to sleeping on the ground. He could feel the tension in his stiff muscles that had come in the night following the disturbing visions. He found Big Bear sitting at his kitchen table with Ben seated with him. Big Bear sipped tea while Ben looked outside the window, deep in thought. He suspected he wasn't the only one that received some sort of messages through visions the night before. Jack joined them at the kitchen table, unsure if he could share what he had seen and felt. He wondered exactly what it was the spirits had tried to communicate. He wondered if it was even the elders that had come or someone else, something else maybe. He knew he didn't want to trouble the young man more than he needed. He already had enough to deal with. *No*, Jack thought, *best to figure this out on my own.*

Jack sat on the Bayview dock, waiting for the ferry so he could once again return to the place he had always called home. In silence, he watched the steady pulse of the blinking beacon of the Oakwood Island lighthouse. He sat, deep in thought about the previous evening and strange things he had seen.

Was that a vision he'd experienced, or had he dreamt it? He was certain he had seen it during the pipe ceremony when he had tried to access the crow's sight, but he didn't remember if he actually managed to get to the crow. He wondered if maybe the crow itself had initiated this exchange again. It was possible, this he understood since he had experienced it in recent weeks.

Either way, the things he had seen reminded him of what this was and made him pay attention to the message it carried. As he had suspected for a long time, it was an evil that was affecting many lives. The same evil that had caused so much death and chaos on the island five years earlier, and for decades before that.

Yet, knowing that it was evil and that it had to be stopped, he didn't really know what to do. There was only one obvious way to end the curse and that was to kill the ones that carried it on. Norah, but also the twins as well. He remembered how he lost his chance years ago when he couldn't bring himself to do it. He had walked out of Norah's hospital room, unable to do what he felt had been his responsibility. Regret had started to build up ever since the deaths had started again. Regret that grew greater since the twins were born.

He knew it wouldn't be an easy task for him and he didn't want to kill a child, let alone two. He knew it wouldn't be something he could live with. He was con-flicted, but he also knew that he had a responsibility to carry out justice for people like Ben Augustine, who might never walk again. He had to end the curse. Many had already died because of the cursed twins and the evil had to be stopped before it gathered more strength and killed again. He felt like he was the only one who could do it. He had hoped for clear answers, but found himself just as confused as before. The only thing he knew for sure was that he needed to sever the tie between whatever evil was at work on the island that had a grip on the young twins.

Glancing at the passenger seat of his truck, Jack recalled the vision he had the previous night after the pipe ceremony. Was the spirit of his grandmother here with him now, he wondered. Was she helping him or was she only being used by the evil itself in order to make Jack do its killings too? She had shown him the little boy with no eyes. The little girl had come to him in the vision and right after he had seen his grandmother torn to shreds.

If there was an answer in these visions and sightings, he knew it had to do with the twins. He would have to come up with his own answer, as he had more questions now than before.

He felt confident that the sightless boy was a sign and that his grandmother had been the one who had told him so. But how could he know for sure? Had the vision been real? Was it just a nightmare brought on by his worries and questions? Distraught, Jack embarked on the ferry. His return to the island would be troubled, but before he stepped foot on the island, he would make his final decision on how to stop this evil curse, no matter the cost.

Chapter 11
Back Yard Feast
Mid July

Sitting on a bench in his backyard, Scott Cudmore sorted through a pair of laundry baskets containing hundreds of socks as he watched Gavin play in the shaded sandbox. It was the first time since the June worm incident that the melodramatic boy seemed happy to play in the sand. Today he hadn't hesitated, taking his favorite toy dump truck and loader in the box and had begun digging right away.

The Davis brothers, Peter, Clay and Colin, were inside along with two of their friends. The group was sitting at the kitchen table playing Dungeons & Dragons. It was one of the only other activities that interested them besides video games. Roars of laughter could be heard every once in a while from the opened window.

Lily sat on the grass next to the sandbox doing what she loved doing most: destroying Barbie dolls. She had random parts of six different naked dolls laid out between her legs. She smiled with glee as she pulled the hair out of one doll's head, a few strands at a time.

Wearing his large sunglasses, Patrick sat on the bench, next to Scott as he felt his way through a Braille children's book. The librarian had said the Braille books Scott ordered were far too advanced for a boy his age. Scott knew better though, as Patrick was significantly mature and intelligent for a four, nearing five-year-old. Both twins seemed advanced, but Lily was very moody and didn't speak much unless it was to her twin brother. Although she did mutter to her dolls when she thought no one was listening.

Scott and his wife Miriam often discussed the twins seeing a counsellor again like they had in the past. It wasn't easy for a little girl like Lily to grow up having a twin brother who needed so much special attention. They also knew it wasn't easy for Patrick to grow up with a twin sister who was mean to most other children, except him. Patrick was soft hearted, a complete opposite to Lily.

Scott had argued that if they saw a counsellor again, they might end up having to go back to the orphanage, which Scott didn't want. His fears fueled enough fear in them both to avoid having the twins questioned by any professional. So far, nothing major had occurred, except the odd behavior Lily exhibited with her dolls and having her head in the clouds sometimes. If something serious were to happen, or if there were signs of something wrong, he would get them help. This he would do in a heartbeat, no questions asked.

Scott had dedicated his life to helping other foster children like himself. That was one of the endearing qualities that Miriam had first loved about her husband. His dedication to the children was amazing to her. She had always tried to bump into him during his visits to the hospital with some of the children from the orphanage. Most orphans never wanted to go back to the orphanage, once they were old enough to get out of the system. Scott though, unlike the others, didn't want to leave. He bought a big house nearby and worked for the orphanage as soon as he was able to do so. He worked there full time until he and Miriam married. Then he became a stay at home father, taking care of foster children like he wanted someone to take care of him when he had been a child.

The first few troubled wards the couple had taken in were still with them. Samantha now seventeen, sat under the oak tree chewing on her necklace while reading as she often did. Bradley, now fifteen, and crushing on Samantha, sat next to her.

He'd been trying to impress Samantha, even to the point of agreeing to read the first Harry Potter book when she had insisted he read it. Amazingly, he'd quickly taken a liking to the book.

Both had been troubled as youths, but stability had turned them into amazing teens that Scott and Miriam were proud of. Children, who used to need constant supervision, now sat quietly reading books.

Scott slowly made progress in matching the hundreds of socks into pairs for the ten people who lived under the one roof. He dug to find matching socks, putting them together and then transferring them to the second hamper.

"Socks, socks, and more socks," Scott muttered.

"Can I help?" Patrick asked with a slight grin.

Scott chuckled slightly as he wondered if the blind boy was sincere about matching socks he couldn't see. Then he thought about it.

"Sure, you can help. I'll dig them out and you fold like this," Scott said as he took the boy's tiny hands and helped him roll a pair of socks together. He moved some books and placed a laundry basket on the other side of Patrick, showing him where to put the socks once folded. Scott proceeded to dig out pairs and hand them to the boy who gladly rolled them up like Scott had shown him and placed them into the basket. He held out his hands as he waited for Scott to give him another pair. The boy smiled wide as he and Scott folded socks together.

Lily glanced over at her brother who seemed happy while folding socks and paused in her destruction of a doll for a moment. A small smile spread across her lips. The only thing that made her sincerely happy was her brother's happiness.

Then Gavin screamed.

Scott had become so engrossed in the act of folding socks with Patrick that he hadn't been watching Gavin as closely as he felt he should have. Looking over at the sandbox he saw Gavin frozen in fear, a wet spot on the front of his pants showing he had peed himself. Otherwise the boy looked fine. He was staring off into the back yard at something. Movement caught Scott's attention and he noticed a porcupine had wandered into the back yard. This wasn't just any porcupine, as this one looked like it had been chewed up and spit back out. The quilled mammal was bleeding from many gaping wounds and was missing much of its face, exposing glistening bone. The small animal seemed to stagger towards Lily as it lurched a few steps forward and staggered to the side. It screeched as it stepped towards the four-year-old girl, the quills that remained on its mangled body leapt to attention, standing straight up on the animal's torso.

Samantha tossed her book aside and scooped up Lily before anyone else was able to react, all frozen in shock where they sat. Samantha hadn't hesitated. While she had jumped in between the porcupine and Lily, Samantha had gotten numerous quills in her right arm. While clutching Lily tightly, she winced from the pain in her arm but still moved to plant herself between Gavin and the small, yet dangerous animal, protecting them both from harm as best she could.

Gavin screamed a second time as everyone watched a pair of large, deformed rats emerge from the brush on the edge of the back yard. They boldly walked to the dying, quill covered mammal. Together, the pair of rats pinned the animal and began chewing on the live porcupine, tearing off bloody flesh and eating it. The porcupine, now pinned to the ground, twitched and convulsed as the predators tore him apart. A third massive rat emerged from the brush and quickly scurried between his two feasting friends and Samantha. Bradley, as if awoken from his trance, rushed to place himself between the seventeen-year-old girl he crushed on, and the strangely mutated rat, which was the size of a raccoon.

Scott stood from the bench wanting to go protect the children but hesitated as he heard Patrick call out for him.

"Scott?" the sightless boy said in an alarmed tone. He wondered if he had left him alone. "I'm scared."

"Get the kids inside," Scott said to the teens he often counted on for help.

The largest of the rats stepped towards Bradley and stood on its hind legs. Samantha took a step back, grabbed Gavin by the hand and moved backwards towards the house. Bradley turned his attention to Samantha for a moment as if unsure what to do next. When he turned to face the rat, he saw its neck had jutted forward and with its mouth open in an unnatural way, the rat sprayed his face with a hot, sticky and rancid liquid. Bradley wiped at his face with his hands and shirtsleeves as he staggered back, blinded by the liquid the rat had sprayed. He tripped over the edge of the sandbox, falling into the sand and nearly landing on top of Gavin's toy loader. He brushed the sticky mess from his face with a sand covered hand as he felt a sudden weight on his torso. He opened his eyes and with blurred vision he saw the large rat had pounced on him and was now sitting on him as it hissed directly into his face.

Bradley screamed.

Scott swung an old rake at the rat. He slammed the rodent across the yard, and it landed with a thud. But the rat did not appear affected in the least. It boldly got up again and hissed at everyone in the yard. It then scurried back to join the other rats who were feasting on the now dead porcupine.

Clay, Peter and Colin had come running outside, along with their two friends. One of them still had his dice in hand. The commotion had been heard from inside the house and they were curious as to what was going on. They stood at the back door, unsure if they should go any further. Scott, noticing them, called out:

"You boys go back inside and open the door when we get there! Make sure none of these rats get in the house!" The boys looked at each other and filed back inside one by one. They watched from the kitchen window, out of the way, while Clay held the door handle, waiting.

Scott helped Bradley to his feet, and they both ran toward the house. Scott peered back at the rats, expecting them to attack. He held the rake like a weapon, ready to swing at the animals again, if needed. Clay swung the door open as soon as they all reached the house. Bradley stumbled on the stairs but managed to get inside with the rest of the kids, followed by Scott, who locked the patio door behind them. He watched the largest rat as it stood up on its hind legs, watching him watch it. Chills coursed over Scott's body as he went scrambling to find one of the many cordless phones scattered about the house. Finding one atop the breadbox, he went back to the door to keep an eye on the rats only to find them all gone. The three rats were nowhere to be seen. The dead porcupine was also gone, realized Scott. The rats must have taken it with them.

Scott listened to the chaos of the house as both Patrick and Gavin cried; Samantha, who was struggling with the pain of porcupine quills in her arm, shouted instructions to Bradley to wash his face. Lily sat on the kitchen floor, sullen and still, tearing the hairs out of a doll's head. Clay, Peter, Colin and their friends stood at the windows, searching for any sign of the rodents. Scott looked at the cordless phone in his hand and tried to decide who to call first. Should he call 911? Should he call cops, forest rangers, or pest control? Then it hit him. He would call his wife. Miriam would know what to do. She always did.

Chapter 12
Deadly Fungus

Detective Burke had a curse of his own in the form of selective memory. For some reason he forgot some things easily while remembering others in vivid details. He always forgot things like his ex-wife's birthday or their wedding anniversary. That was one of the many reasons she was now his ex-wife, however most case details always stayed with him as if burned into his mind forever. Especially the ones that remained unsolved. This had irritated his wife, as she thought this meant Burke's personal life was less important than his work. Even though that was true, Burke couldn't choose what remained in his memory. He didn't get to choose that.

Like the autopsy pictures of Ryan McGregor and the subsequent autopsy results, there were certain things his mind would never let go. He was thinking now about the autopsy results as he stood in front of the late officer's gravestone. Ryan, a native of Oakwood Island had lost his life on the job while trying to protect the very island he loved, and so had been given an elaborate tombstone to honor his service. His final resting place was decorated with an ornate granite piece with police cruiser lights carved into the top of the gravestone.

"Bravery is not the absence of fear
but action in the face of fear."
Ryan Robert McGregor

Burke adjusted his glasses and lit a cigarette using his Zippo as he tried to forget the images of Ryan's mangled body. The doctors had tried to patch him up and stop the bleeding, but the wounds had been too severe. He had already lost too much blood, and there had been no saving the young officer, as much as they had tried. Burke tucked his lit cigarette between his lips, the smoke swirling around and into his nostrils as he patted his pockets in search of his now ringing cell phone.

"Burke here," he said, placing the phone to his ear.

"The amount of data you guys have based on the small samples collected from the crime scenes and bodies is amazing," Jin Hong blurted. He hadn't bothered to say hello when Burke answered, getting right to the point.

"This is a mutated strain, from what I can tell. It has to be the same as what we found in Peru. But I can't understand how this fungus got all the way to this remote island across the continent."

"I don't get what's so hard to understand? I mean, if you could find it in Peru, why not here?" Burke asked. "If you can find something in one place, then why is it so difficult to imagine it being found in another place?"

"You don't get it," Jin replied. "This thing survives in Peru only because of the conditions, the climate."

"But you said it yourself," Burke replied, pausing to take a drag from his cigarette before he spoke again. "It's a mutated strain. If it evolved, then why couldn't that help it survive in a different climate? It could adapt and survive, right?"

"Fine," Jin replied, who wouldn't admit that Burke had a point. "But what boggles my mind is this: what are the odds of this thing being on this island and being found by someone like Danny, who knew what he was looking at in the first place?"

"True," Burke replied. "You got me on that one."

"Did you talk to anyone about what I asked you?"

Instead of answering right away Burke lit another cigarette off the first one, before crushing its tip between yellow stained fingers and pocketing the butt. He then blew out smoke from the fresh cigarette. "Not yet," he finally replied.

"You still don't think they'll agree to do it?" Jin asked, annoyed.

"Look. Exhuming multiple bodies for an active case is one thing, but to do that to look for mould on cases everybody wants to forget is another thing altogether."

"Fungus. Spores. We'd be looking for spores."

"Look, I don't think that will be necessary as something tells me that you're going to find much fresher samples anyway."

"What makes you say that?" Jin asked.

"Back when this shit all started, we had found dead animals scattered on the island. Most of them appeared half eaten. I'm thinking if we had known what we were looking for at the time, we probably would have found the same traces on them as we did on Ryan, Maggie, Danny and the other bodies too." Burke looked at the smoke curling up from the cigarette.

"I've asked local forest rangers, cops, the local vets to hang on to any dead animals they find for the next little while, especially those that look like they've fallen victim to predators. That way we can get samples and you can run some tests."

"You can still do that?" Jin asked. "While still on sick leave?"

"They don't know that. Plus, they know me."

"I still think we should exhume at least one body. If we do find new evidence on the animals like you say, then we can compare it to the old findings to see if it's evolved even more. We can see if the body is still contaminated or if my theory is right."

"What theory?"

"Well, they found traces on that cop, Ryan, when they did the autopsy. Traces that survived on him after being treated at the hospital, I have the reports. I have to wonder if the strain died off in the confines of a coffin or if it mutated still."

"Mutated?" Burke asked. "What do you think we'll find in that coffin, friken zombies?"

"Actually, I don't know," Jin replied. "But I'd love to find out."

"Let me call Randolf and run this by him to see what he thinks."

"Randolf?" Jin replied. "The coroner?"

"Yes. Exhuming bodies would be something he would know more about than me since I've never had to do it before. Although I think when I tell him why, he will tell me I'm crazy, which is not that far off from the truth, you know."

Both men had an uncomfortable laugh before ending the call.

"Fuck!" Burke exclaimed as he jerked his hand as he felt the cigarette burn his fingers. He looked at his hand and the cigarette was gone. He saw it smoldering on the ground and watched it for a brief moment before stepping on it to put it out. He picked up the butt and put it in his pocket with the other one. He'd throw them away later when that wouldn't mean desecrating a grave to do it. Lord knows, if Jin has his way, he would be desecrating a grave or two soon enough, he thought.

Jin wiped sweat off his brow with the sleeve of his t-shirt as he pocketed his cell phone and knelt to tie his sneaker. He tugged at them making the bow tight. He locked the Bayview Rental SUV he had used to get to his destination and turned to face the thick forest before him. He took a paper map of Oakwood Island from his back pocket and unfolded it. The map had red dots on it, marking places of significance. Like where the old trailer was where they found all the bodies. Another dot in town noted where they had found the dead body of the young woman they originally thought to be Norah Jenkins. With help from Burke, Jin had made a dot for every place they had found evidence of the fungus he now hunted for on the island.

The coroner and local law enforcements had dismissed the idea that this spore could have anything to do with the bizarre happenings on Oakwood Island, past or present. Jin needed more evidence to substantiate his theories. Of course, Burke believed him, but the detective's credibility was on a slippery slope already.

Jin had theories about Maggie's supposed suicide, most of which he hadn't even shared with Burke yet. How could he tell Burke he thought the spores were what had killed Maggie? He had no way to prove she didn't kill herself like everyone thought she did, by throwing herself off the hospital's roof. Even though she had the largest number of spores collected than any of the other bodies they had found. Nobody had even considered that her suicide was connected to the spores. Jin needed more to prove his theory that the spores had something to do with everything that was still happening. Perhaps the dead animals would contain proof like Burke suggested, thought Jin.

Right now, he knew what he had to do and that was to get strong evidence.

The first place he wanted to check out was where Danny's remains had been found. According to the chambermaid, Danny had plastic bags containing what was most likely evidence. Since those samples were thrown out, he didn't know for sure, but it made sense that Danny had known about the fungus, perhaps the location of his remains would hold additional clues. Why would he have been there to begin with? Perhaps it was the location of more samples of the fungus.

Many thoughts raced through Jin Hong's mind as he slipped on a small backpack which contained everything he had picked up for his hike: latex gloves, a dust mask, a box of Ziploc bags, marking pens, bug spray, a small first aid kit, water, and some granola bars. He also had some red fiberglass tape, which would do in a pinch to identify important locations. The clerk at the store also strongly suggested he bring a canister of bear spray. The bear population on Oakwood Island wasn't very large but enough to warrant bringing a can, just in case, insisted the clerk. Jin had said he didn't want it at first but eventually reconsidered. He wished he had his work gear, which included a small portable lab, but what he'd managed to gather would have to do. He used an app on his phone to mark his location. Then using a compass app, he got his bearings before beginning his trek into the thick forest of Oakwood Island.

Hours later, Jin sipped water as he wondered how he had gotten lost. He hadn't remained lost for very long as Jin was very good at reading maps, plus he had used the app on his phone to trace his route. But he *had* managed to get lost. He had been too preoccupied in taking in all that he could, looking for anything that might not belong in a temperate deciduous forest. If the zombie ant fungus was found here, maybe something else normally native to the Peruvian Amazon might also be found on Oakwood Island. Danny had made the place sound mystical the week before he had left for his Cousin Gertrude's wedding. Jin had seen and heard a plethora of critters and birds so far but nothing that seemed out of the ordinary. Plant life here was typical to the climate, nothing stood out to him at all. *Am I on a wild goose chase*, he wondered?

Jin looked at the app on his phone again then put the water back in his pack. He pointed himself in the direction where the location of Danny's death had been marked on the app and continued his hike. He continued to check the app, trying to not get turned around again, and a while later the app indicated that he was at the spot.

Jin looked around. The only evidence confirming the location where Danny's remains had been found, other than the location on the GPS app, was a piece of yellow police tape still wrapped around a tree branch. It fluttered in the slight breeze as Jin reached for it, instinctively wanting to pocket what he thought of as litter, adding it to the half-dozen items he had already collected during his hike. But Jin changed his mind as he thought this marker best remain where it was, for the time being anyway. He looked around but the location where Danny's remains had been found turned out to be completely bare of any obvious trace of spores and showed no sign of anything abnormal.

Disappointed at the lack of any spores, Jin used his cell phone to take a picture of the police tape wrapped around the branch. He wanted to document everything, and this would help prove where the spores were located he thought. He looked at the picture to make sure it was good enough and noticed something in the background of the image he'd just taken; an odd shape on a branch behind it. At closer inspection, he thought he saw what resembled a face of some type of animal. The more he zoomed, the more blurred and distorted the subject was. Looking up from his phone, he scanned the trees where the thing would have been and saw nothing. But the shape in the picture was there. Jin held the phone up while examining the trees behind the piece of yellow police tape trying to match the image on the phone. He saw the same branches but the lump that looked like a small animal in the picture wasn't anywhere in sight.

From behind him, a sudden rustling sound startled him. He spun around quickly, to see what had made the noise but there was nothing there. He couldn't help but remember all the town gossip of werewolves and monsters in the shadows as he looked about for any signs of life but saw nothing. A new rustling sound came from behind him yet again. He spun around again, now facing the tree with the yellow police tape. Jin thought about digging out the bear spray when he spotted a pair of squirrels leaping from one tree to the next, as they exploded in loud squirrel chatter in the process. One squirrel chased after the other as they darted up one leafy maple tree only to leap to a branch of another nearby tree. The pair of combative squirrels chased each other out of hearing distance. Jin was relieved to find it was squirrels and not a werewolf stalking him as he looked at his arm to see gooseflesh. With all the stories of werewolves and dead animals being found, Jin found himself more nervous in the forest of Oakwood Island than he had ever been in the Amazon of Peru.

Old wives' tales, thought Jin as he saw what looked

to be a clearing in the trees up ahead. He made his way towards it with renewed determination, forgetting his paranoia of monsters in the shadows. Stepping through thick brush, Jin emerged in the small clearing only to step into something mushy. He stepped aside, hopping on one leg trying to see what was now under his sneaker. A gooey black slime clung to the shoe. Jin looked at where his foot had landed and saw a puddle of blackened mush. Jin leaned closer to what he now realized were guts. Small animal guts were in a blackened pile on the ground before him.

The part that struck Jin as strange was that there were no flies. Not a single one. A small pile of entrails like this should be covered in flies and yet it was not. Using his cell phone, Jin took a couple of pictures of the strangeness before him. He scrapped his shoe on the root of a tree trying to get the gunk off as he checked the quality of the pictures. Satisfied with the images, Jin turned his attention to the small clearing and froze in his tracks. Just above him, dangling from a tree branch was a decomposing rabbit. Suspended on the branch by its mouth, the dead rabbit dangled with its stomach completely burst open with a few small pieces of entrails still dangling from the gaping hole. Jin quickly assessed that the puddle of blackened guts he had stepped in had once belonged to the dead rabbit dangling above him.

"No fucking way," Jin exclaimed as he took a step back while lifting his cell phone to take a picture of the rabbit. As he took the picture, the sole of his gut encrusted sneaker slipped out from under him, making him fall backwards, hitting his head on something hard in the process. Stunned, Jin felt the back of his head and looked at his hand expecting blood but found none. His head hurt but perhaps the blow hadn't been as harsh as he assumed.

Unsure if he just hadn't felt the correct spot, he propped himself up on one elbow and ran his other hand over the back of his head again and still saw no blood. As he looked at his hand, Jin realized that he had dropped his cell phone when he fell.

Before Jin could sit up, something pounced from the shadows and landed on his chest, knocking him down flat again. A large, deformed rat sat on his torso and before he could react, it hissed and sprayed a sticky, slimy substance into his face. Jin ineffectively wiped at his face with a bare forearm and tried to blink away his now blurred vision. The weight on his chest left as quickly as it had come.

Jin struggled to his feet and stumbled backwards while using the sleeve of his t-shirt to wipe at his eyes, trying to remove the slimy substance. Something rustled in the tree above him. Something else rustled on the ground before him. He looked up, trying to see through the burning pain in his eyes. Jin's legs began to tremble as bile rose up from the twist in his stomach. More rustling seemed to come from all around him. Jin turned away from the noise and ran as fast as his blurred vision allowed, stumbling through the brush. Jin stumbled in a clumsy run until he tripped over a tree root and crashed forward. Disoriented and panicked, Jin pushed on until a pain in his side made him stop. He felt his pockets for the cell phone until he remembered he had dropped it somewhere back where that thing that sprayed him. Where the dead rabbit hung in the same way the infected ants had hung once affected by the spores. The rat-thing had spit slime in his face, a gooey pus like substance.

His eyes continued to burn, and he used what little water he had left to try and wash the slime off. He heard more rustling in the forest and he fumbled in his backpack for the bear spray. He pulled it out as he heard a rustling sound, pulling the cap off he tried to spray towards the noise but with slime on his hands, the can slipped from his grasp. Jin panicked as he heard more rustling and ran in the direction he thought his rental car was parked.

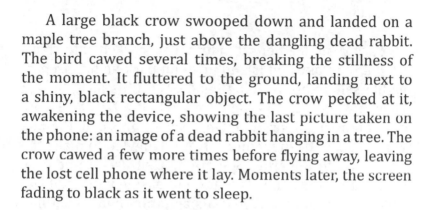

A large black crow swooped down and landed on a maple tree branch, just above the dangling dead rabbit. The bird cawed several times, breaking the stillness of the moment. It fluttered to the ground, landing next to a shiny, black rectangular object. The crow pecked at it, awakening the device, showing the last picture taken on the phone: an image of a dead rabbit hanging in a tree. The crow cawed a few more times before flying away, leaving the lost cell phone where it lay. Moments later, the screen fading to black as it went to sleep.

Chapter 13
Hounded

Jack Whitefeather sat in his truck, parked at the back of the Oakwood Island hospital parking lot, preparing himself before heading inside. With his head bowed down, his long grey hair and brown hat hid his face from any potential passerby, giving the impression that he was asleep. In deep meditation, he struggled to make the connection to the crow. Something that used to be easy for him to do was now getting increasingly difficult. He couldn't help but wonder if his agitation had something to do with it. Jack was experiencing real stress for the first time in his life. Always a confident man, Jack had done what needed to be done without worrying about the consequences. Most often the things he needed to do could be done in secret. However, this time, the path he felt he had to take involved killing a child, and this was a decision he struggled with even if he had always known that it might eventually come to that.

Jack left the truck and snuck into the hospital to check on Edwina Quartley, who had been seriously injured just the day before. Jack needed to know if his fears about Edwina's injury were correct. He headed to one of the upper floors and found Edwina's room. He saw Pete Quartley at the bedside of his comatose mother, talking to a nurse. Jack slipped into the room to listen in.

Edwina Quartley had been a teacher until a nervous breakdown had forced her to give it up. She had found a second career as a mail carrier and had served the island for twenty-six years. Edwina had taken her job very seriously and had done it with zeal. She had loved every aspect of her job, except for the mean dogs. She'd been bitten as a child, and after being bit on six different occasions, she would suffer panic attacks before her shifts. Her fear had a hold of her. She'd find any excuse to not deliver the mail to any house with a dog in the yard. She was on the verge of losing her job, and so Edwina had begun carrying a pocket full of dog treats. She used the treats to bribe and befriend all the dogs on her route, and soon after doing this, her fear of dogs had been abated. She'd overcome her fear and gained the loyalty of the dogs on her route, even the ones other carriers said were to be avoided. Any new dogs on her route would be quickly won over with the help of a pocket full of tasty treats.

This ritual had recently failed her with one particular dog, a mix of some sort of pit-bull and Rottweiler. It was a large and particularly mean dog that seemed immune to her treats. She had been forced to log a complaint about the dog that she simply hadn't been capable of bribing.

When Scott Cudmore had gotten the call from the post office about his dog, he had been confounded. He had argued with the post office manager, explaining that there had to be a mix up as he had no dog. But the manager had insisted that the mail carrier had seen the dog on the front porch of the Cudmore home with a little girl. She had only seen the girl at first but as she had approached the steps, the dog had appeared at the girl's side. It had barked at the letter carrier with such ferocious intensity that Edwina's

123

bladder had reacted without her knowing it at first. Her fear of dogs had been abated but apparently not cured.

A few days later, Edwina had issued a second complaint; the dog had been outside, unattended and untied when she had seen it. It hadn't barked but had growled and stalked her. She had thrown four treats its way, hoping to win over this beast of a dog. She had slowly started to back away as the canine stared at her with an intensity that made Edwina leave with the Cudmore's mail still in her hand. The treats she had thrown at the dog had been completely ignored as it had watched her with a disturbing glare.

A third and last complaint was logged in with her manager and another call to the Cudmore residence made. She had been relieved to see that nobody appeared to be home and no dog was in sight on this particular day. She had approached the house, looking at the front porch, her ears waiting for the slightest hint of sound. When none came, she went up the steps, and looked into her mailbag for the Cudmore's letters. She dropped several envelopes in the mailbox that was mounted near the front door. She smiled as she heard the wind chimes in the breeze. Looking up at them, she saw an open window upstairs. She noticed a flutter of light brown hair and movement and heard a little girl's giggles. Stepping down the front porch steps, she kept her eyes on the upstairs window, wondering if it was the same little girl she had seen on the porch the other day. She had thought nobody was home, but maybe she'd been wrong.

As she took a few more steps, her eyes never leaving the upstairs window, she heard movement coming from the right corner of the house. A quick rustle came in the grass, fast movement rushing towards her. She knew before she looked. Her worse fear was rushing towards her at full speed. As soon as she set eyes on the dog, she could have sworn its eyes glowed bright red. The dog barked loud as she started to run down the front walkway. She hurried as best she could with the large mailbag she carried. She ran all the way down the Cudmore's yard, looking back once. She saw the dog gaining ground and behind it, the little girl stood on the porch, laughing.

As Jack sat unnoticed behind the divider curtain in Edwina's room, the nurse told Pete Quartley that witnesses saw Edwina running from the Cudmore house as if she was being chased. Edwina had been looking behind her as she ran, as if something was nipping at her heels but the witness said there was nothing chasing after the mail carrier. In her haste, Edwina had run into the road and stumbled into the path of an oncoming vehicle which struck her, sending the mail carrier rolling off the hood and into the opposing lane only to be run over by a second passing car. The driver of the second car, who had been distracted by his cell phone, had run over Edwina's legs pinning them to the road. Edwina had screamed at the top of her lungs, blood spraying as she shouted. The witness said she had been shouting "Get it off me!" repeatedly until she had succumbed to her injuries and passed out.

Everyone now thought the comatose Edwina Quartley had lost her mind. Everyone except Jack Whitefeather. Before coming to the hospital he'd found out from one of the Cudmore's neighbours that the little girl had been watching from the porch and laughing at the woman as she ran away, just before she was struck by both cars. Jack was sure the Cudmore girl was the reason behind the mail carrier's critical injuries. Evil had a grip on the little girl and Jack was the only one who knew about it. He was the only one who had a chance to stop it, to prevent things like what happened to Edwina from happening to anyone else.

He had to stop this madness for everyone on this island who called it home, for the greater good; he had to do what was necessary.

Jack slipped out of the hospital room unnoticed.

Back in the cab of his truck, Jack Whitefeather's meditation felt like it was finally working. He saw a blurred image in his mind of a patch of tall grass which he didn't recognize at first. Then the crow shifted its gaze and Jack saw a large oak tree in an open field that he recognized instantly. The bird was on the back of his property. The tree he looked at through the crow was the tree his mother had planted over the grave of his grandmother, Sparrow Whitefeather. The otherwise unmarked grave had remained undisturbed since his own mother's passing.

Before the tree, a shimmer appeared, and Jack knew even before the vision was clearly visible that it was his grandmother's spirit. This was the Sparrow he now remembered as a child, an old frail woman, with gnarled hands and few teeth remaining. She wore the same dress she had worn in her youth, the light brown one with the burn mark on her chest. The old woman extended her arms towards the crow, palms up, fingers splayed as if inviting the bird, or perhaps him, to come to her. The spirit of the old grandmother opened her mouth wide as if chanting, but no sound came at first. Then Jack heard the sound coming from inside his mind, the sound of rushing wind which would eventually carry a keening voice along with it. The crow launched itself into flight.

Jack's body convulsed as in his mind's eye, he saw the bird fly headlong at Sparrow Whitefeather's spirit. In an instant, the bird was flying into the old woman's wide-open mouth and Jack's body stiffened as everything in his mind's eye went black.

A flash came to him of a circle of fire, followed by another flash of the twins, standing in the center. He heard his grandmother's stern voice commanding him to do the unimaginable. *What was this circle of fire? What did it mean?* He thought as the visions came.

"Kill the children! Kill the children and end the evil bound to their family!"

Jack's body tensed, knocking his hat against the back window of the truck making it fall off his head. The voice of his grandmother echoed once again in his mind, louder than before.

"The boy is a sign! Kill them and end the plague of evil twins forever!"

Why is the boy a sign? A sign of what? Jack wondered.

His hand immediately covered his ears as Jack woke from his trance. He was soaked with sweat and tears immediately welled up in his eyes. *But what of Norah*, he thought as he felt a pain in his chest and panicked. He clutched at his chest and grimaced. It was like nothing he had ever felt before. Was this the day he died, he wondered? A heart attack would save him from what he needed to do, but it wouldn't save others from the evil that clung to Lily. Jack took a deep breath and felt the pain in his chest subside. Was this what real stress felt like, he pondered. He needed to relax. A heart attack might be a blessing in disguise for the old man but not for the future victims of the Jenkins' curse.

Chapter 14
Generations of Evil
Year: 1917

Nineteen-year-old Fannie Jenkins sat in the nursery of her new, secluded home, built for her by her former lover, Edmond Finley. He had made a lot of money in the flourishing lumber industry of Oakwood Island. With wood from his mill and money to pay for the construction he had built her a beautiful home, telling people it was what a good and responsible Catholic man did, help someone in need.

With twins of her own of little more than two years old, Fannie found herself thinking dark thoughts again, like she had done during her youth. She had struggled with a darkness inside her throughout her childhood and never understood why. While pregnant the darkness had seemed to subside and she felt like perhaps she could after all, finally lead a normal life.

The courtship with Edmond Finley had been shortened by the unexpected pregnancy. In one of her episodes of darkness, as she liked to call them, Fannie had seduced the good Catholic Edmond. This had not been a problem for Edmond, until he learned that Fannie was pregnant with his child out of wedlock. His Catholic upbringing had engrained in him the thought that a child born out of wedlock was sinful. His parents and family would shun him if they learned of Fannie's pregnancy. Edmond ended the courtship before Fannie showed any signs of the pregnancy to protect his reputation and he'd secured Fannie's agreement to end their relationship by vowing to build Fannie a home for her and her child.

Fannie though, had had twins and it wasn't long after the children were born that the rumors began to spread as people speculated on whom the father really was. Several people were sure it was Edmond, but other stories spread of how her brother was the father. Those rumors had been fueled by Edmond in order to protect his own reputation. He would recount the scandalous story to anyone who would listen, and added that he'd known all along, which was why he'd built Fannie the house to protect her from her evil brother. Having provided for Fannie and the babies financially, he had been seen as the hero in all this in the end. He knew he was the father, but he would never correct any of the rumors. What he did not know was that rumors were based on a truth he would never fully comprehend.

In 1914, on their parent's farm and cattle ranch, Fannie and Liam, her sixteen-year-old twin brother, had been growing more independent. Fannie's parents had kept her and Liam sheltered for a long time, never wanting to let them venture out too much. She knew there was something about her that her parents were afraid of, ever since she had been a young girl. She had always felt – *something* – deep inside of her, something dark, and Fannie suspected that this was why their parents had been so overprotective.

But eventually, as the twins got older, their parents had become more complacent in their discipline. Wallace, their father, was getting older and needed help on the ranch so when Fannie and Liam had become teenagers Wallace had put them to work on the farm and ranch. The new experiences had been liberating for a time, and Fannie and Liam soon learned that by completing their work that they had gained some independence from their parents.

This all changed one fateful night when Liam and Fannie both experienced something so traumatic that it would mark them forever.

One day one of their father's business associates had come to the ranch. He was from Anchor's Point, the small village on the mainland, and he'd brought along his daughter to see the ranch. Liam had been working near the house when they'd arrived, and the girl had laughed when they first met. This caused Liam to feel uneasy and self-conscious, but he was smitten with her beauty and long, blonde curly hair.

The blonde girl came to the ranch several times over the course of that summer. Every time she would giggle and laugh whenever Liam was around. Liam eventually grew tired of the laughs and giggles. He assumed she was laughing at him, which annoyed him, but he wouldn't show it, as he was attracted to her. Unbeknownst to him, her giggles were simply due to her being nervous around him, a young man, she too found very attractive.

As the laughing and giggling continued, Liam's growing lust for the girl became fueled with anger.

For some time, Fannie had thought her darkness had been under control. She'd gone several months without having had an episode. But one night that summer, the darkness came to her out of the blue. As always happened when the darkness came, she did not try to change her thoughts, nor did she try to stop them. She felt a sense of longing for the ultimate control she knew she would have over the person in her midst. It was like she had no control over herself during her episodes, but she could control those around her, in the most intense and often-times scariest of ways. With this power, Fannie could do whatever she wanted and had done so since she had been very young. She used it to her advantage a few times to scare Liam with the sight of a snake in the tall grass. He would run off, terrified of the slippery serpent. She would laugh, amused at this power to frighten her brother as well as others around her. Although she didn't know how it happened, or where it came from, she didn't push against it either as she loved the thrill she felt whenever it happened.

On this particular evening, the only other person nearby happened to have been Liam. They had been tasked with cleaning the barn. As her thoughts turned towards her brother, everything in the barn dissipated around her. She could only see him and nothing else while she could feel something, a presence of sorts, taking over. She felt the desire welling up inside of her, the wanting to control, to use it to her advantage. Her lips curled at the corners, a smile spreading across her face as she stared at her brother.

Liam had stopped sweeping and looked up towards Fannie. There, standing in front of him, was the blonde girl from the mainland. Surprised but happy to see her, he smiled as he propped the broom against the nearest wall. He looked behind her to see where Fannie had gone, but could see no sign of her anywhere. He cleared his throat, wanting to talk to the pretty young woman standing in front of him.

"What a nice surprise to see you here! I thought you were back on the mainland. What are you doing here?"

He saw her smile at him, her bright blue eyes so inviting. He felt himself blushing, his excitement obvious at the sight of her. Just as he was about to ask her if she had seen his sister when she came in, she let out a slew of giggles. Liam's smile vanished just as quickly as the giggles started. As he watched her, his skin grew warmer as she began laughing hard, pointing at him while doing so. She laughed and jeered at him as she undid the top buttons of her white blouse, exposing the soft skin of her perky breasts. As he watched her undress slowly, still laughing at him, anger filled him alongside a desire that he could no longer hold back. He rushed to her, ripping apart the rest of the buttons of her shirt, grabbing her breasts and kissing her hard on the mouth. Pushing her down on the hay in the corner of the barn, he had his way with her, the blonde girl laughing the whole time, moaning in pleasure in between laughs. Once he was done, he collapsed on her, panting from the excitement and release of his first sexual encounter. As he raised himself off though, he realized the blonde girl was no longer laughing, nor moving. Looking down, he saw his sister, Fannie, eyes wide in fear and shock, pulling down her skirt and closing her ripped blouse with shaky hands. Without a word she ran out the barn and to their home up on the hill.

No one would ever know that Liam thought he was with the girl from Anchor's Point. Not even Fannie. Though she knew the darkness that overcame her could bring about much trouble and pain to those she inflicted it upon, she understood very little about the evil that poured out of her when she was affected by it. She had no control over what happened when it took hold of her.

She only knew that she often felt this darkness envelop her, creating evil thoughts that scared, yet excited her. This time however, it had cost her a lot more than what she had bargained for. The same dark thoughts would eventually drive her family away.

Once at the house, she had run up to find her father and told him that her brother had attacked her in the barn. After her insistence, Wallace had confronted Liam. The boy claimed he hadn't been with Fannie, but with the girl from the mainland. He admitted that he had been intimate with the blonde girl, but somehow Fannie had appeared out of nowhere, and the other girl was gone. His father knew better. The girl Liam liked had gone back to her home on the mainland a week before.

When Wallace explained to his daughter that Liam had been confused, that he was convinced she had been the girl from Anchor's Point, Fannie knew something strange had come over her brother, and it was her own doing. She knew that when the darkness came over her, her thoughts would focus on someone and drive them mad, drive them to see things that weren't really there. She knew she couldn't tell her parents this, or anyone else for that matter, as no one would believe her.

Wallace and Hester feared for their children's sanity, as they both sounded mad, like Henri, their real father, had been before hanging himself years ago. Wallace decided to send Liam away for the rest of the summer, trying his best to keep the twins separated. He hoped that distance would allow them to regain a sanity they both seemed to have lost.

But after Liam was sent away, Fannie had started spending more time in town, trying to escape the dark thoughts. She had met Edmond, and had seduced him, not knowing if it had been the darkness or her own desire to escape the events from the barn.

When it was discovered that Fannie was pregnant, and Edmond had ended his courtship, Wallace feared that Fannie would be driven completely mad. As the rumors spread among the townsfolk, he was sure that Fannie would go crazy, but she'd seemed unusually calm. When Edmond agreed to build Fannie the home, Wallace thought it was a good thing, despite the rumors he knew Edmond had been spreading about Liam. The home seemed to provide Fannie with some stability that had been missing in her life. But throughout her pregnancy, Wallace feared for the safety of her unborn child. Would it be born with this sickness of the mind too? Would it suffer at the hands of their mother, or its uncle?

Now, a few years later, as Fannie sat in the room where her twins slept, she idly wondered if the children had her ability. Would they be able to taint someone's mind? Would they get a thrill from the darkness when it came?

Was she going even madder by thinking about this? Maybe she wasn't really going mad at all, but instead being driven into madness by her own children. She wondered; could such evil be passed on?

Chapter 15
Better That Way

Jin Hong opened his eyes and saw stars in the night sky above him. He felt the cold ground beneath his back, and an ache that spread from his shoulders all the way down to his lower back. His vision blurred, the stars becoming fuzzy glows and then his eyes regained their focus and the stars turned into sharp pointy pin pricks of light again. He turned his head, pounding and heavy, and saw trees jutting out of the ground on each side of him as he came to the realization that he was still in the forest. Feeling disoriented, he wondered how he got there and how long he had been lying there. The last thing he remembered was running. Why was he running? Why were his eyes burning? Confusion had its grip on him, and he couldn't seem to gather up his thoughts in a cohesive manner.

He heard a rustling sound nearby and noticed a part of the darkness moving. Jin felt panic rise in his chest and a scream build in his throat. A scream he suppressed as he realized the patch of moving darkness was a large black bear a few feet away. The bear approached him slowly until he could feel its breath on his face, sniffing out his scent. Tears ran down the sides of his face from a combination of fear and the burning sensation in his eyes. Jin held his breath in anticipation as the bear sniffed at him before it turned and walked away. Jin would later think he heard the bear's stomach growl as he lay there, holding his breath while it inspected him. He wondered why the bear had not killed and eaten him but was relieved the bear had decided against having him as a meal.

Jin sat bolt upright when his memories of events flooded his mind. He remembered the disfigured rat leaping onto his chest and spraying something in his face and eyes. He patted his eyes which felt free of the sticky substance now but still felt hot. Jin touched them and felt slight swelling. He looked about for the bear and saw that it was gone. Jin patted himself down, assessing the situation as if expecting to find injuries. His backpack was gone and so was his cell phone. With no compass and no flashlight, he would have to navigate by stars alone. As Jin got to his feet and tried to look up at the stars, he staggered and reeled from a momentary head rush. Pain shot down his back and across his shoulders, but he managed to regain his balance. He continued his assessment of himself. Besides the pain from the fall, he realized that the only other injuries he had were a sore scalp and the burning irritation in his eyes. He studied the stars and decided he was confident enough that what he was looking at was the Big Dipper and the North Star. He got his bearings and began to walk. He must have passed out and that's how he ended up still in the woods at this hour, he thought to himself. With a combination of his aches and pains plus the darkness he soon stepped on a tree root and rolled his ankle and fell on his side.

This is going to be a long damn walk, he thought to himself as he got to his feet and began his trek again but this time with a slight limp. He still managed to bend tree branches to mark his path. This much he remembered from his training as a scout, long ago.

After what felt like the longest hike of his life, Jin was back at his motel room. He felt exhausted. His head ached and his entire body shook with fatigue, but he couldn't rest just yet. Not until he made a call. The trek through the dark woods guided by what few stars he could see had taken Jin much longer than he had anticipated. During his long journey back to the motel, he had nothing but time to ponder the predicament he knew had befallen part of Oakwood Island. He had no idea what that rat thing had been, but he knew what that dead rabbit was.

It was very bad.

The way the dead rabbit hung from the tree from its maw with its guts opened meant the fungus was spreading. It was spreading on a scale that no one had ever seen before in creatures much larger than the tiny little zombie ants he studied in the Amazon forests of Peru. *Burke won't believe me*, he thought as he dug through paper files trying to find the business card the detective had given him.

A short time later, Jin was lying on the bed, a soothing wet washcloth over his itching eyes and the motel phone at his ear.

"You know what time it is?" he heard Burke say through a voice hoarse from too many cigarettes. "Who is this?"

"It's Jin. I lost my phone, so I called you from the motel phone."

"It's 4:37... AM. Couldn't this have waited until the morning?" Burke asked.

"It is morning," Jin replied. "I have something to show you."

"Now?"

"Fuck! The picture's on my phone and I lost that," Jin replied. He hadn't thought straight since waking up in the woods hours ago. Jin heard a rustling sound, creaking and then a flicking noise come from the phone.

"Are you smoking?" Jin asked as he patted the damp washcloth on his face.

"No," Burke replied, followed by a cough he tried to muffle.

"Anyway," Jin replied, knowing Burke was lying about smoking in his motel room which was non-smoking. "I found evidence that the fungus is still on Oakwood Island. And it's worse than I thought."

"We'll have to bring that to a lab to run tests."

"Actually, I didn't get physical samples. I wanted to but something weird happened and I kinda ran for my life."

"Look, maybe it's just really late and I'm really very tired as I don't sleep well anymore but... did I just hear you say you had to run for your life?"

"Yes, it's a long story that you probably wouldn't believe anyways. But the things I saw, you need to see it yourself to believe it." Jin replied.

"Well, honestly, the only way to have anyone take us seriously is to get samples to Randolf so we can confirm your theories, so we know what we're dealing with here."

"Look, about that," Jin said. "I'm not so sure I want to do that anymore. Not after seeing what I've seen." Removing the washcloth, Jin swung his legs out and sat on the side of the bed. He squinted at the television cable box to read the time as he tried to focus. His eyes still stung but not as much as before which pleased Jin. He didn't have time to deal with that as there were more pressing matters at hand.

"I'm too tired to ask, but why the fuck not?" Burke replied. Jin could hear the frustration in his voice rising.

"I've always had a feeling this was something the government big wigs would love to get their hands on. Make a weapon out of it. But I wasn't too worried about that until today," Jin replied. "You didn't see what I saw."

"No, I didn't," Burke replied with a sigh. "But without evidence, how am I supposed to convince people that this case isn't over. That the deaths of a lot of the people are still open cases while they look for killers that might not actually exist. I want answers and if this mould shit of yours gets me the edge that I need..." Burke said before Jin cut him off.

"Look. Nobody... and I mean nobody wants to study this more than I do. It's my life's work. But I made a promise to myself long ago that if I ever thought this could be turned into some sort of weapon by power hungry people..."

"Let's resume this conversation in the morning," Burke said, sounding more tired than when he answered the call.

"Fine," Jin replied. "Get some sleep."

"You too," Burke said with exasperation.

Jin didn't bother explaining that he had already had a long nap that day. In the woods. He had no idea why he had passed out. But now he had an idea of what had to be done. He simply couldn't let this flourish. He had a lot of evidence in the files already. He could always collect a few biological samples before he did what he now felt had to be done. He would safely store them away for his own research later on. Nobody needed to know about those. He could study them before letting anyone know about them. It would be better that way, he thought.

"You remember Jin?" Burke asked Shelley as he took a seat at the counter at the Old Mill Restaurant which was starting to fill with the daily regular lunch crowd.

"The plant guy who worked with Danny Nolan?" Shelley asked.

"Yes, the plant guy I had pie with," Burke added, reaching into his pocket for his cigarettes before remembering that he wouldn't be able to smoke in the restaurant.

Shelley passed a paper order to the cook before grabbing a cup and coffee pot for Burke. She set the cup down and filled it quickly, spilling a bit of coffee in the process. Shelley was ramping up to lunch rush mode as she grabbed a cloth tucked into her apron and wiped up the spill. She folded the cloth, using a clean section she continued wiping the counter, putting a little extra effort on that stain that would never come out, yet she'd try every time she saw it.

"What about him?" Shelley inquired.

"I was supposed to have breakfast with him this morning," Burke replied as he sipped hot coffee. "I overslept," he added. "It's past eleven and he's not at the motel."

"Well he hasn't been in here today," Shelley replied with a sharp tone. "You need a menu?" she asked.

"I'll have the usual," Burke replied, who meant his everyday order of two eggs, bacon, pan fries and toasts.

"Breakfast special ended at eleven. You sure? It'll cost extra."

"Sure, why not," Burke replied as he drank the rest of his coffee and held up the empty mug to signal Shelley. "And if you do see Jin, tell him to call me."

"I'll make you a deal," Shelley replied as she handed Burke's order to the cook. "I'll tell Jin to call you, if you tell Grady to call me... if you see him. Jerk just up and walked out on me about a half hour before you got here."

"He quit?" Burke inquired.

"He didn't say a word. Just walked out the front door and kept going."

"Told you he was an idiot," Burke replied with a sly grin.

"Well if it makes you feel any better, he didn't look so good when he came in this morning and he looked even worse when he left."

"Why would that make me feel better?" Burke asked as he watched Shelley grab a few plates of food and head off in the direction of a table where an elderly couple sat together. The old man seemed to say something to the old woman and then spoke to Shelley as she laid the food before them. Burke noticed the old man kept glancing in his direction.

"I love small towns," Burke muttered as he reached for his cigarettes again but decided he would wait until after the meal.

Chapter 16
Who Died?

"Hey there," Miriam said as she greeted her husband in the almost empty waiting room of the Oakwood Island Hospital. He sat in a chair with Patrick sitting at his side, feeling his way through a Braille children's book. Lily sat two chairs away from Patrick, having a staring contest with one of her partially dismembered Barbie dolls. The naked doll was missing one arm, one leg and part of its hair.

Miriam, in full nurses' uniform, glanced at Peggy Martin who sat with a wet towel covering her face and an older woman sleeping in a wheel chair in the corner of the otherwise empty room. When she was confident that no one was watching, she leaned in, kissing the still seated Scott on the lips.

As if he could read his wife's mind, Scott told her exactly what she wanted to know, "The boys are at daycare for a bit while the rest of us take care of a few things." Scott was referring to the four other children that were not present. "Bradley saw the doc. He says the drops seem to be working but if his eyes are not better in a couple days that he will get him to see a specialist. Samantha's with the doc now. I think it's getting infected," Scott added, referring to the porcupine quill injuries Samantha had gotten while protecting the children.

A nurse walked in and spoke in a soft voice to Peggy Martin, who removed the towel, got up and followed her out of the waiting room.

"She's an amazing kid, that one," Miriam said to Scott. "I'm so glad you insisted on taking her in," she added, referring to when Samantha was seven and very troubled.

"I spent my childhood in that orphanage, around kids like her." Scott left out the part where Samantha reminded him of his fellow orphan and friend Maggie. "I knew she was smart and also recognized her need for love and stability," Scott said as if it was nothing special.

Miriam smiled at Scott as she spoke, walking backwards as she did. "I'll call you later to see how everything went." She spun around, walked away with quick steps, needing to get back to her duties.

Scott smiled to himself as he watched the woman he loved, even more than his foster children, walk away to get back to her job of helping people. He turned his attention to little Patrick who hid behind his large sunglasses while feeling his way through his book. Scott turned and saw that the chair where Lily had sat was now empty. She wasn't there. Scott's heart sunk and panic set in when he glanced about the room and didn't see her.

"Lily?" he said aloud as he stood and looked to see if she was behind chairs and simply out of sight.

"Come," he said to Patrick as he scooped up the boy and walked out of the waiting room. He glanced up and down the hallway, watching an old man being wheeled into a room by a bearded, male nurse.

"Lily!" he said in firm yet hushed tone. Down the hall, he saw something that looked familiar on the floor. He walked briskly towards it, still carrying little Patrick in the process. Standing over what he confirmed to be a plastic Barbie doll leg, he knew the little girl had been through here. A feeling of panic rose as Patrick struggled in his arms.

"Down," Patrick said.

Scott, in his state of growing panic was about to deny the boy's request until he remembered the bond between the twins. If Patrick wasn't panicked, Lily was probably fine. It was a crazy idea but it was also tested and true so he would need to trust the boy. *But the question is, where the hell is she*, he thought?

Patrick searched and found Scott's hand, grasping it in his.

"There," the blind little boy said pointing to the elevator as he began walking towards it with his head cocked to the side as if in concentration, as if listening.

A helpless feeling washed over Scott as he followed, letting the boy lead him. Scott wondered if the boy knew what he was leading him towards.

"The elevator?" Scott asked. He couldn't help but wonder how the blind boy would know this. The bond between these special twins had always been a little abnormal, and sometimes it scared Scott, something he had never told a soul, not even his wife. He was about to scoop up the boy when he paused. Patrick extended his hand and stepped forward until he touched the wall. He felt for the edge of the elevator door, ran his hand up and down, side to side until he found the button and pressed it. Scott stood there befuddled, unsure what to say or do.

When the elevator doors opened, Scott heard the soft muzak inside. *The Girl From Ipanema* played softly as Patrick pointed inside.

Was it the music? Did Patrick hear the music from the waiting room, wondered Scott, as he stepped inside the elevator with Patrick.

"Two," Patrick said confidently.

"Are you sure?" Scott asked. The music he could understand as the boy had incredible hearing. *But how would*

Patrick know which floor, Scott wondered as anxiety bubbled inside him.

"Two," Patrick repeated as he stood waiting, as calm as could be.

Scott reluctantly pressed two and watched as the doors to the elevator closed and the soft muzak played on. *The second floor is the Daye Psychiatric Ward*, thought Scott. When the doors opened, Scott felt a momentary relief as he saw the plastic arm of a Barbie doll on the floor up the hall. He scooped up Patrick and briskly walked to it. Confounded, he looked about before looking at Patrick who had guided him this far; a feeling of helplessness coming over him as he wondered which way. He stepped forward but stopped as suddenly as he had started. Which way? He walked up the hall and paused at the bend, glancing back the way he'd come, just in case. Down the hall, he saw what he now realized he knew he would see. A lock of hair from the Barbie doll lay on the floor, the trail the little girl had left them. Was it intentional? It was just like the time she had hid in the pantry. A similar trail had led Scott to her then as well. He wondered about this as he marched forward with Patrick still in his arms.

"Lily!" he said softly but firmly.

Patrick cocked his head to the side like he did when listening intensely, he pointed toward a bend in the hallway. Scott looked at the blind boy, wondering if he heard her. He walked to the end of the hall, rounded the bend and saw a confused looking Samantha standing behind Lily. Samantha glanced back at Scott as a tear rolled down her cheek.

"Mommy," Lily said pointing at the door before her. "Mommy's dead."

A visibly shaken Samantha stepped backwards, as if to get away from the little girl.

Scott marched down the hall, handed Patrick to Samantha and pushed open the door before them.

"Miriam?" Scott blurted.

In the room, he saw a disheveled woman with matted brown hair in a hospital gown bound to a bed by restraints often used with difficult patients. She had multiple I.V. lines in her arms. The room was bare of anything, but the necessities required. A simple night table next to the bed contained a box of tissues and a glass of iced water. From his vantage point, Scott could see the bathroom door ajar and the room empty. The only one in the room was the woman in the bed. Scott stepped closer to see the woman's chest wasn't moving. *She isn't breathing*, thought Scott. He looked back at Lily who stared at the patient in the bed who had a stone blank expression. Scott rushed past Samantha who was brushing away her tears with a bandaged arm as she cradled Patrick, hugging him closely. Scott rushed down the hall and stopped a nurse as she walked past.

"I think she's dead," Scott blurted, taking the nurse by surprise.

"Who?" the nurse asked.

"There," he pointed. "In there," he added as he led her to the room down the hall.

Samantha took Lily by the hand and gently pulled her away from the doorway, letting the nurse enter the room.

"Mommy's dead," Lily repeated to anyone who would listen.

"She's ok," Miriam said as she pulled down her pants and sat on the toilet of the public bathroom, her cell phone clutched to her ear.

"I know," Scott replied as he spoke on his old cell phone. He glanced down the hospital lobby watching Samantha and Bradley who were taking the twins out the front entrance. "But it scared the shit out of me."

"She's fine," Miriam repeated in an effort to calm her husband down. "And to answer your question, the woman who died, that was Norah Jenkins. She used to be a nurse here are the hospital until she lost her mind."

"So..." Scott started.

"So yes, she was Lily and Patrick's mother."

"How would..." Scott began.

"I don't know. Maybe she overheard someone say something," Miriam said, referring to Lily knowing that Norah was her birth mother.

"Are you sure?"

"Yes," Miriam replied. "I don't need adoption records to confirm it either," Miriam added as she stood, pulled up her pants, flushed and exited the stall. "She used to work here. And she had her twins here." Miriam eyed herself in the mirror as she continued speaking to Scott.

"At first, they thought she was having twin girls, but it was discovered that the initial ultrasound had been done with a faulty machine, and so it was not accurate at all. Even Norah thought she was going to have two girls until she gave birth. It was quite a surprise, apparently."

Miriam heard Scott sigh on the other end of the line. She wouldn't mention how it annoyed her when he did this, but she quickly brought the focus back on topic.

"Plus with Patrick's condition, people talk."

"If it's such public knowledge, why didn't I know who Norah Jenkins was?" Scott asked with a sharp tone in his voice.

"I'm sure the orphanage wanted it kept quiet and it was at first, but Patrick being born like he was, it was sure to get someone's attention at some point," Miriam said, referring to some of the articles and television coverage that had come and gone.

"That's certainly true," Scott replied as he remembered the reporter who begged him to call when the kids started school so he could do a follow up story on Patrick, the boy with no eyes.

"And just so you know, I wasn't sure the rumors were true which is why I never said anything about it."

"You should have told me," Scott replied. "If you knew."

"I didn't want it to change the way you looked at them. If you knew their mother was in the psych ward, you might have over thought their eccentricities."

"I wouldn't have," replied Scott who later would think that he answered that too quickly. Perhaps knowing might have made him question some of their strange behaviors. He wouldn't admit it, but he knew his wife was right for not telling him.

"Anyway, we'll talk later," Scott said. "The kids are waiting for me outside."

"Love you," Miriam said as she heard the phone go dead. It wasn't like Scott to end a call without telling her he loved her, thought Miriam. Lily wandering off like that must have really bothered him. Or maybe it was him thinking she had died. Or perhaps it was not knowing about Norah Jenkins. Small communities have many rumor hubs; sometimes coffee shops or restaurants where people gather, sometimes a local pub or bar. Other times the hub can be a workplace like a hospital, which employed a lot of island residents. And you didn't always know if the rumors were true either.

She pocketed the phone and washed her hands as her mind spun in multiple directions. Yes, she had heard the rumor long ago that Norah was their mother. She had also heard that Patrick and Lily were the results of experiments in genetic manipulations. Another one was that they were twin embryos from a lab that were placed in different mothers to be conceived. There were too many crazy stories of the boy born with no eyes and his twin sister who many said was born with no vocal cords since they had never heard her speak. This she knew wasn't true even if the little girl was very quiet; there was nothing physically wrong with her. People in small communities talked so what part could one believe for sure, pondered Miriam as she went back to work.

Peggy Martin sat on the exam table in the emergency room of the Oakwood Island Hospital, wet towel in hand. She spoke without hesitation when Doctor Kingsley walked in.

"Who died?"

"What?" Doctor Kingsley inquired as he marveled at the chart as she was the second patient with irritated eyes within the hour.

"Who died?" Peggy Martin repeated. "I overheard someone saying something about somebody dying."

Doctor Kingsley ignored the question and got to the point. He was busy, impatient, and didn't have time for gossip. Besides, he would have heard if someone had died in the hospital while he was on duty.

"What seems to be the problem?" Doctor Kingsley inquired as he took a small flashlight from his pocket and put a hand under Peggy Martin's chin to steady her head while he looked into her eyes. Peggy Martin assumed he had read her chart and knew about the gunk she got in her eyes while taking out the trash. What Peggy Martin didn't know is Doctor Kingsley was also checking to see if she was on drugs.

"What happened here?" Doctor Kingsley repeated.

"I was taking out the trash and something sprayed me in the face. It got in my eyes too," Peggy Martin blurted, stating the obvious. "It happened so fast I don't know what it was. It burns, Doctor Kingsley. I think it might be infected. At least that's what it said when I Googled it," Peggy Martin added. She wanted Doctor Kingsley to know that she already knew she had an infection.

"Yes," Doctor Kingsley replied. "I see that," he said as he continued examining her eyes. "Well whatever it was you got in your eyes, it doesn't look like it did any damage but it sure did cause irritation. There's no infection yet," Doctor Kingsley said, contradicting his patient's self-diag-nosis as he pocketed the flashlight and grabbed something from the table behind him and began looking into Peggy Martin's ear. "But you need something to prevent it from getting infected and to help with the itching. I'll prescribe some eye drops for starters."

Doctor Kingsley felt Peggy Martin's neck, checking glands, further assessing her condition.

"I have such a hard time with those," Peggy Martin replied. "I blink too much. And leaning back makes my sinuses run down my throat and makes me gag a lot. One time I threw up too. Google talks about it being something wrong with my sinuses but I don't want any operations."

Doctor Kingsley bit the inside of his cheek, trying to not say what was on his mind.

"Keep using the cold compress as much as you can," Doctor Kingsley said, gesturing towards the towel Peggy Martin held in her hands. He turned and scribbled on a prescription pad. "It will help with the itching. But get this prescription filled as soon as you can. If it's not better in a couple of days, come and see me." He handed her the paper, smiled his best bedside manner smile, stepped back and opened the door of the room to find a nurse standing there.

"Cindy?" Peggy Martin blurted, pausing when she realized she couldn't remember Cindy's last name.

Both Nurse Cindy and Doctor Kingsley turned to look at Peggy Martin who spoke quickly.

"Cindy, who died?" Peggy Martin asked impatiently.

"Oh," Nurse Cindy replied in surprise to have Peggy Martin asking her this. "Someone in the psychiatric wing passed away," Cindy added, earning herself a look of disapproval from Doctor Kingsley. Cindy knew she wasn't supposed to say anything. You don't want family to hear about a loved one's death through rumors and gossip.

"Get that prescription filled," Doctor Kingsley replied. "And next time you're not feeling well, come and see us." Doctor Kingsley left out the part where he wanted to tell Peggy Martin to stop consulting Dr. Google.

Chapter 17
The Gift of Sight

The morning light ushered in through dirty windows as Jack sat in his cabin in the woods on Oakwood Island. He sat crossed legged on the floor, his head bowed down and his long grey hair hiding most of his features. Before him was a small clay bowl containing a smoldering sweet grass braid. Small tendrils of smoke floated around him. He chanted in a low, muffled voice that could barely be heard, had anyone been there to hear it. The crow had returned to him the last few days as if all was normal again. Because of this, Jack felt a renewed sense of determination for what had to be done. He felt that the crow was an omen. When he had a difficult time communicating with the crow, it had left him thinking he was on the wrong path. Perhaps his intentions were wrong. *Perhaps they will do more harm than good*, he thought.

He had to end the curse of evil which had befallen the twins and been handed down through generations. *This cannot be allowed to continue, for the well-being of everyone the twins encountered*, he thought. The clarity with which he saw through the crow was better than ever. His ease of communicating to it that morning had put his troubled soul at rest, at least for the time being as he sensed he was doing what had to be done.

"Be my eyes, old friend," he had told it a short while ago, much like he had many times before. Like before, the bird seemed to know exactly what he wanted. It had flown high above Oakwood Island, finding what it sought. A single spirit unlike the others it saw. The island Jack saw through the crow contained many troubled spirits, most were harmless wandering souls, beyond help. But some held more sway on the living and had intentions. The one he sought now he thought had intentions, but he knew not what kind or how much sway it might have at this point.

The crow swooped down and landed on the branch of one of the many weeping willow trees on the hospital grounds. Through the crow's eyes, Jack saw the spirit of Sparrow Whitefeather as she watched four young children as they waited outside on a park bench in the late morning sunlight.

Jack recognized the Cudmore foster children right away; the two older teenagers who were often caring for the much younger twins, Lily and Patrick. The spirit of his Grandmother seemed stronger than ever, shimmering as she approached the children. But before she could reach them, a new spirit came to be, between her and the children.

Jack's physical form, seated in his cabin, jolted slightly at the sight of the new spirit.

Norah Jenkins' spirit was faint and seemed to shimmer with a multicolored aura, something Jack had only seen a few times. The multicolored aura, he believed, meant her spirit was tainted. During his recent visit to the hospital, he had been told that she had pneumonia. He recalled something about fluid in her lungs but now wasn't sure. Whatever the cause, seeing Norah's spirit Jack knew that Norah had died.

Sparrow's shimmering spirit pointed to the little girl who sat on the bench, looking at what was left of her doll, a torso with a now bald head. The spirit of Norah Jenkins raised her arms before her with the palms of her hands facing outwards as if she was warding off Sparrow, to protect her children.

Through the crow, Jack saw Scott Cudmore exiting the hospital entrance. The older children, who were oblivious to the spirits around them, began gathering Lily and Patrick as they prepared to leave. Jack focused on the pair of spirits and saw that both of them were now staring directly at him somehow; as if they could also see through the crow, seeing him where he sat in a trance-like meditation. Norah's spirit held a hand out, palm up, as if in invitation for Jack to come to her. Sparrow Whitefeather's spirit pointed at Lily and gave Jack a stern look.

Jack's meditation broke suddenly, as if he'd been shoved out of the mental link with the crow. He found himself sitting on the floor of his cabin. The small clay bowl of incense before him was crushed, as if someone had stepped on it. Broken pieces of the bowl were covered in the ash from the burnt sweet grass.

Next to the bowl was something that had not been there before. Surprised, Jack picked it up and looked at it closely. It was a rib bone that had been carved and sharpened into a dagger. He remembered the weapon from his youth, having seen it in his grandmother's home. Sparrow had kept it on a high shelf, a memento of something that she never bothered to explain to Jack. It had been packed up and stored away with all her belongings when she'd died. Now it was here.

Jack glanced about, noting that his windows and doors were still closed. No one had been inside while he meditated. An uncharacteristic shiver ran down Jack's spine. Something was warning him.

Chapter 18
No Time to Waste

With his pants still on the bed, wearing his dress shirt, underwear, and socks only, Burke sat at the desk in his motel room, flicking cigarette ashes into an empty soda can as he held his old cell phone to his ear. The phone on the other end of the call rang on but no one answered. Burke ended the call as he heard the voicemail pick up yet again on what was his third try in the last hour. He had hoped that by now, Jin had found his cell phone and he would be able to reach him to find out exactly what he was up to.

Burke put his cell phone in his breast pocket and pulled out a folded piece of paper. Unfolding the paper, Burke scanned it over, desperately looking for a potential clue he might have missed the other times he had read it. The note must have been wedged in his door when he left that morning. Perhaps it had been tucked under his door. He wasn't sure, but he had missed it. He found it pinched into the door when he returned to his motel room, after lunch at the Old Mill. He had to have closed the door on it when he left as that was the only way it could have been in the door the way it was. Then again, maybe it was the chambermaid who put it there, he thought as he looked at his cigarette with a twinge of guilt for smoking in a non-smoking motel. He was getting rusty, his best detective days behind him.

The paper contained no other evidence and so Burke

pushed up his glasses and read the note again.

Burke

Meet me at Ocean's Edge Road near the Stuart's house. You'll see my SUV parked on the side of the road near the place where Danny's remains were found. Meet me there and hurry. There are things you need to see for yourself to understand why this is more important than solving an old case.

There's no time to waste as I need to do this now before it's too late.

Jin

It was obvious to Burke that Jin felt strongly about this. Burke was obsessed with solving the pile of mysteries from this damned island. Jin had also wanted to solve many of the same mysteries but now he spoke of dangers that were of greater importance than solving past crimes, no matter how brutal. The longer Jin remained on Oakwood Island, the more convinced he was the fungus was spreading. The more convinced he was that it was becoming a real threat to all life on the island.

Burke put on his pants in a rush, zipped them up and grabbed his keys and shoved the note back in his pocket. As he was rushing out the door, Burke remembered an old saying his mother had used many times when he was growing up.

"Time to shit or get off the pot," Burke said aloud. With the motel room door closing behind him, his cell phone started ringing. He answered it without hesitation.

"Jin?"

"Are you out of your friken mind, Burke?" Coroner Harold Randolf blurted excitedly. "You want to exhume decomposing bodies to look for mold?" The coroner had obviously received his message requesting exactly that.

"Not me... Jin Hong. He's a plant scientist that used to work with Danny, the dead kid. He's got a Ph.D. in eco-physiology or some shit like that."

"More like eco-dum-ass-ology if you ask me," Harold Randolf blurted, clearly frustrated. "If you think I'm going to go to the families of the deceased and ask if we can dig up their loved ones to look for mould because a former detective who's half out of his mind and his sidekick are asking me to, you've seriously overestimated our friend-ship."

"So, is that a no?" Burke asked with a slight grin as he flicked the ash from his cigarette and took a drag. "Hello?" Burke added as the line went dead. "I guess that's a no then."

Chapter 19
God Help Me

Scott Cudmore sat at his rolltop desk while speaking to his father-in-law on the phone. Miriam's father, Reverend Nathanial Masterson, was a descendant of brothers who were some of the original settlers of Oakwood Island. Scott, an atheist, didn't exactly see eye to eye with his father-in-law on the topic of religion. While Reverend Masterson thought very highly of Scott Cudmore, a man who dedicated his life to children in need, he thought Scott should go one step further and enroll the children in Sunday School at his parish church. Scott had refused to do so as he believed that religion should be taught as part of history and not a belief system. For that reason, they always tried to skirt the topic of religion and spoke of everything else, but not that.

"Miriam told me about the porcupine incident," Reverend Masterson said, referring to Samantha's injuries.

"Doctor Kingsley gave her antibiotics and a cream for the itching," Scott replied.

"And Bradley," Reverend Masterson inquired. "Is he any better?"

"It's not gotten worse," Scott replied. "Miriam is going to talk to Kingsley about that specialist he told us about. We're thinking he should see the specialist as soon as possible."

"I'll be praying for them, son," the reverend replied out

of sheer habit before quickly changing the subject. "How are the twins?"

Scott always dreaded this question. The good reverend had actually been against Scott and his daughter taking in Lily and Patrick. As a man of God, he preached doing good for his fellow man and loved that Scott did this, helping as many orphans as possible. However, he felt that the twins needed too much. He was afraid that the burden would be too great for his daughter to bear. Unlike Scott who was a full-time caregiver at home, Miriam had a demanding full-time job which heaped a lot of responsibility on her, above the caring for orphans at home as well. As a father, he worried about the well-being of his daughter.

"The twins are fine," Scott replied. "As fine as they can be."

"Miriam told me what happened… what happened at the hospital."

"They're fine," Scott replied with an air of annoyance. He knew his wife couldn't keep anything this significant from her father. Especially not something the town's folk would gossip about. The death of former nurse Norah Jenkins reignited the rumors of her being the biological mother of Lily and Patrick. A rumor that Scott now believed to be true, mostly because when he asked about it at the orphanage, a few of his old co-workers skirted the subject, but nobody actually denied it.

"Scott?" he heard someone say. Scott pivoted his chair and saw Samantha standing by the patio door. "You know that old guy that lives in the woods?"

Scott pulled the phone away from his mouth but kept it pressed to his ear.

"Jack Whitefeather. What about him?"

"He's parked out front and he's staring at us. It's giving me the creeps," Samantha added, her eyebrows up high and her eyes wide in fear.

Scott got up from his desk chair, walked to a front window and peered outside. He saw Jack Whitefeather's truck parked on the opposite side of the street before his house.

"Can I call you back?" Scott asked the Reverend but didn't wait for a response and ended the call. He turned back to see that Samantha had gone back outside to watch Lily, Patrick, and Gavin who were playing in the sandbox. Clay, Peter and Colin were still in their bedroom playing their video games. He could hear them chattering as they clicked away on their controllers.

Why was Jack Whitefeather parked in front of his house? He recalled a discussion between him and his wife about Jack once. Scott was convinced that Jack was narcoleptic. How else could anyone explain him being seen sleeping in his truck all over town. Maybe this was what was happening now. Maybe Jack had been napping in his old Ford and had just woken up but was too groggy to drive so was waiting until he felt up to the task. *Maybe that is it*, thought Scott. But he was watching them. Watching the kids, from what Scott could see.

Jack Whitefeather isn't one of those creepy guys who goes after kids, Scott thought. While Jack was a strange one, Scott knew that Jack never hurt anyone unless they had it coming. There were a few stories about Jack, rumors mostly. Of how the old man often knew things he shouldn't and how he was almost always present during or shortly after horrific and tragic events that happened on the island.

A chill went up Scott's back as these thoughts coursed through his mind. What if Jack knew about these things *before* they happened? What if he was here because something was about to happen to his family? What if that was why he was watching them?

Scott shook off the chill and dismissed these thoughts as crazy. Scott didn't believe in magic or superstitious crap. He clipped the cordless phone to his belt, went outside and walked across the street towards Jack's old red truck.

Jack locked eyes with Scott as he watched him approach.

"Can I help you, Jack?" Scott asked.

"You know who I am?" Jack Whitefeather inquired.

"Everyone knows who you are, Jack. It's a small island."

Jack frowned at the thought that he stuck out that much. The residents of Oakwood Island were few in numbers, sure, and he did have a distinct look about him, he supposed, which was why he preferred to do his watching through the crow, on most days.

Jack pointed to the house across the street. "That's where Ben Augustine had his accident. Fell off the roof."

"The old Ketchum house," Scott replied. "He was working on the roof and fell. I remember. The new owners are moving in soon, I think."

"Mr. Ketchum had a heart attack in that house, didn't he?" Jack asked, still looking at the house across the street from inside his truck. He sat up straight in his seat, the adjustment making it creak in the process.

"Yes. Tragic thing. Barely had time to enjoy the place," Scott replied.

Jack turned his attention to Scott who was glancing back at his house and then turned his attention back to Jack.

"Mrs. Ketchum had a stroke there too, didn't she?"

"Yes," Scott replied. He was now starting to wonder if Jack was insinuating something about the old Ketchum house.

"And right there," Jack pointed to the street right

behind Scott. "Right there is where Edwina Quartley got run over by a car."

"What are you getting at, Jack?"

"Don't you find all that strange?"

"Things happen, Jack. Terrible things, yes but I'm not understanding what this is about." Scott took a step closer to the truck as he spoke and noticed Jack had a shotgun on the seat, the barrel of which was on Jack's lap and it pointed towards the driver side door of the truck.

"Do you know who Norah Jenkins is?" Jack asked.

"Was," Scott replied. He was a bit alarmed that Jack had the shotgun. "She passed away."

Jack nodded his head slowly. Norah was dead, and now Lily and Patrick were the last of the twins afflicted with the curse. With the twins being so young, he could act and end the curse. There would be no one left to have children, ending the lineage of evil. That had to be why Sparrow had come to him now, after such a long time. This had to be why he had visions of her. She must have known Norah would die. A woman who, even though locked in a psychiatric ward had still managed to have children and pass on the evil to her offspring. Would doing this be enough to stem the evil? He didn't know for sure. If he knew it would, he would have done it already. Killing children wasn't something a moral man like Jack could do lightly. With a guarantee of it ending the evil, he could but without knowing, it was a big risk.

"Did you know," Jack asked. "Did you know that Norah had a twin sister?"

Scott was confused by this. He hadn't known much about Norah until recently. If she did have a twin, Scott thought it odd that his wife wouldn't have mentioned it; although she had kept much from him when it came to Norah Jenkins.

"You don't find it strange that all these horrible things have befallen people all around you ever since you took in Patrick and Lily?" Jack asked.

Scott swallowed his nervousness and tried to get to the point at hand. "What do you want, Jack? Why are you parked out here?"

"My grandmother says it has to be me," Jack replied as he laid a hand on the shotgun.

Jack must be losing his mind, Scott thought. *Jack must be seventy at least, so his grandmother can't possibly be still alive. Could she?*

In that moment, a large crow swooped down and landed on the hood of Jack's truck, startling both Scott and Jack in the process. Scott took a few steps away from the truck as the crow cawed twice in his direction. He turned and marched back towards his house as the cordless phone on his belt began to ring. Scott answered the call as he got to his walkway and spun to watch Jack.

"Hello?" he said into the phone while being completely distracted by what he was seeing.

Jack clutched the steering wheel with both hands as he convulsed and tensed in his seat. The crow stood on the hood of the truck motionless as it watched the old man in the truck.

"What the f...," Scott started saying before cutting himself off avoiding the cuss word that he tried so hard not to utter, especially not in front of the kids.

"Hello? Scott? Did you hang up on my dad?" Miriam asked. She knew this was out of character for her good-natured husband.

Jack Whitefeather had been ready to grab his shotgun

and end all this, even if he had to kill Scott too. He had felt a sudden sense of urgency and desperation. He would do it and be damned for it, if those were the consequences. He had felt ready to act until the crow landed and startled him. Before Jack could even question why his feathered friend had come to him so abruptly, the bird had pierced his mind once again.

In the vision he saw a ring of fire, though he soon realized that it wasn't merely a ring, but a pentagram. The pentagram was made of flames, and in its center, he saw a long white bone stuck in the ground, the familiar curved handle covered in intricate carvings. His grandmother's dagger pointed up to the dark clouds. The burning pentagram was in a small clearing near the edge of a cliff. A place that Jack recognized. He had been there before, on one of his many explorations of the island. He knew the place but why was the crow showing him this?

The crow cawed loudly in his mind and his sight snapped away from the clearing and the burning pentagram. He saw himself sitting in his truck. He was seeing through the eyes of the crow and next to him sat Sparrow Whitefeather, only now she was old again. She sat next to Jack's physical form but stared at the crow with a fierce intensity that broke Jack out of his involuntary trance.

Jack awoke with a tightness in his chest which he believed to be a heart attack at first. He relaxed his grip on the steering wheel as he breathed deeply, watching as the crow took flight, disappearing from view.

Jack saw Scott standing on his front walkway, watching him while on the phone. Jack didn't wait to see if Scott was calling the police. Breathing deeply, he felt the pain in his chest subside as he started his truck and drove away.

"Well that was fuckin' weird," Scott blurted to Miriam who was still on the other end of the call.

"What's going on?" Miriam asked. She knew something wasn't normal just by the sound of her husband's voice, even through the phone.

"Scott!" he heard Samantha scream from the house. "Scott!"

"I'll call you back," Scott said to Miriam as he ended the call. "What?" he asked Samantha as he turned and walked to the front door where she now waited for him.

"Bradley left."

"What do you mean, left?"

Scott and Samantha went to the back yard where Patrick sat stacking his blocks into a pyramid. Lily was stripping the clothes of a new pair of dolls she had just received, and Gavin was in the process of digging a hole in the sandbox with his favorite toy loader.

"Bradley wasn't feeling well, so I told him to go lay down. Which he did," Samantha explained. Scott could see she was in an agitated state which he knew wasn't normal.

"But just now, he came out again and looked really pale. I asked him what was wrong, but he ignored me, walked right past me like he didn't even see me."

"Walked right past you," Scott repeated while trying to understand where this was going. That wasn't like Bradley to ignore Samantha. *He idolizes her*, thought Scott.

"He walked right past me and into the woods," Samantha added, pointing to the forest behind the house. The Cudmore house was on the outskirt of town which meant its back yard was linked to a large stretch of woodland.

"Into the woods?"

"He walked off in the woods," Samantha repeated.

"He didn't mention where the hell he was going?" Scott asked in frustration.

Before Samantha could respond to Scott's question, a whimpering sound came from the sandbox where the kids played.

"Worms!" Gavin screamed as he broke into sobs, stood up and wet himself.

"You go get Bradley," Samantha blurted. She was often better at handling Gavin when he was upset. "I've got this," she said referring to the little ones.

"You sure?"

"Go," Samantha urged. "Something's wrong with him. Go!"

Samantha scooped up Gavin in her arms and wiped at his tears with the palm of her hand. Patrick had a confused look about him as he tried to understand what was happening around him. Lily was having one of her staring contests with one of the Barbie dolls she had clutched in her grasp. The naked doll still had all its limbs but already had all its hair torn out.

Scott turned and ran into the woods behind his home. He stopped and peered back towards the way he had come. He already couldn't see his house through the trees even though he had not run very far.

"Bradley?" he shouted hoping for a response that didn't come.

He ran a short distance more but stopped when he saw a familiar running shoe that he knew belonged to Bradley. Surely, he wouldn't be going too far after having lost a shoe.

"Bradley!" he shouted louder this time, letting his frustrations out.

A crow quietly landed on a branch and watched as Scott ran past it. The bird cocked its head in curiosity, much like the blind boy often did. The bird took flight and flew through the trees, towards the direction Scott ran until it found what it needed, as if it had already known it would be there.

A single sock on the ground snagged to the bark of a tree root. While in flight, the crow swooped down, picked up the sock and flew away with it. The bird landed again, watching Scott who had stopped to catch his breath. The bird dropped the sock near a beaten path. It pecked at the sock and cawed twice, as if trying to attract attention to itself.

Scott, seeing the bird pecking at the sock, immediately ran to it shooing the bird away and grabbed the sock. It was one that he remembered Patrick folding, not long ago as he and the boy had folded socks together. Seeing what looked like beaten down foliage before him, Scott ran down the makeshift path a way before stopping to call out for the boy once more. In the distance, Scott heard a gunshot.

Gavin clasped onto Samantha with all his strength as his sobs subsided. Samantha stood next to the shaded sandbox, clutching Gavin to her as she watched helplessly as the old man had returned. He carried a shotgun and stood next to the sandbox. He had appeared out of nowhere while she had been busy consoling Gavin, catching her by surprise.

"I have no choice," Jack said as he reached for Lily's

arm. She scurried away from him in the sandbox before standing up. "Come girl," he called to Lily as he watched Samantha. He wasn't pointing the gun at the teenager as he didn't think he needed to. *She already has a bandaged arm, no doubt caused by the same evil that put Edwina Quartley in a coma*, he thought. *The same evil that put Ben Augustine in a wheelchair and the Ketchum couple in side by side graves.*

"What do you want?" Samantha demanded as she struggled with Gavin.

"I have to end the evil," Jack replied. In his current state he firmly believed that Samantha understood what he referred to. He was now convinced that the entire Cudmore household knew about the evil that plagued the twins. He had convinced himself just now that Samantha knew and was protecting them. *Perhaps this is why the evil had only recently harmed her*, he thought, looking again at the bandages on her arm.

"Samantha?" Patrick muttered in an inquisitive tone. He dropped the blocks he had been clutching in the sand and got to his feet. The boy cocked his head as he listened intently trying to understand everything going on around him.

"Come here," Samantha said hoping Patrick would follow instructions and walk to her voice. "Come to me."

Lily stared at Jack, who was watching Samantha.

Jack saw a dark shadow in the corner of his eye. There was something in the woods. The hairy beast was back as he saw it dart from one tree to the next. In one swift motion, Jack shouldered the shotgun and fired, hitting the side of a tree, sending splinters airborne. Jack glanced at the girl who had dropped to the ground, shielding the other boy with her body. Patrick had his hands cupped over his ears to muffle the sudden explosive noise he had heard. Lily hadn't budged. She stood still, her eyes fixed on Jack. Jack turned his attention to the woods and saw nothing. He looked at Lily and saw a sly smile on the little girl's lips. This was her doing; him seeing the beast that had been haunting his dreams since Ryan's death. It was Lily and not the eyeless boy like he had previously assumed. He had never really been certain until this very moment. She'd removed all doubt from his mind. *She is the evil one and not the boy, but will knowing this help*, he wondered?

The crow landed on a branch of the large oak tree and cawed loudly, startling everyone. The bird put a stop to Jack's brief thoughts of shooting the little girl to get her out of his mind. *Not now, not like this*, he thought.

"Patrick," Samantha said firmly as she watched Jack with growing nervousness. "Come to me, Patrick." She held out her hand while still covering Gavin.

Patrick had pulled his hands away from his ears and turned his head, listening to her instructions but ignoring them.

"I think we have to go with him," Patrick replied. "With the man in the hat."

"NO!" Samantha blurted. She jumped to her feet; Gavin still clutched tightly to her. The desire to protect them all tearing her apart emotionally. Tears ran down her cheeks as she looked at Jack's shotgun and wondered if she could somehow wrestle it out of his grasp.

"Yes, come with me," Jack said. "Come with me."

Patrick with his arms outstretched, clumsily stepped toward the sound of Jack's voice. Jack stepped sideways and scooped up the boy who had no eyes with his free arm, as the other held the shotgun.

A sob escaped Samantha as a feeling of helplessness washed over her.

"Come, Lily," Patrick said to his sister.

"Yes. Come, Lily," Jack repeated as he watched Samantha struggle to keep from crying as she held Gavin to her body with all her might.

Jack walked backwards for a few steps as Lily, with a doll in hand, followed as Patrick clung to the man who carried him.

"NO! Don't!" Samantha pleaded. "Please!"

"It's ok," Patrick replied. "This is supposed to happen. Like the woman said," Patrick added.

Samantha stood in confusion, tears pouring down her face. Jack turned around, carrying Patrick as he marched to his truck. He glanced back and saw that Samantha clutched Gavin and cried while Lily followed him like her twin brother had asked. Moments later, Jack drove away with the twins in the truck as Samantha and Gavin cried in each other's arms.

Scott emerged from the woods, alone, confused, and out of breath. He had planned to keep searching until he found Bradley, but when he heard the gunshot he ran back as fast as he could. As he exited the woods, he spotted Samantha, kneeling in the backyard clutching Gavin while powerful sobs rocked her body. Colin, Peter and Clay were standing around them. They all looked so afraid. Panic rose inside of Scott as he realized not all the kids were there.

"What's going on?" Scott asked as he looked around, searching the back yard. "Where are the twins?" He spoke fast, needing to know where they were. He knelt on one knee beside Samantha and placed a hand on her back in an attempt to calm her enough so she could tell him where the twins were and why she was crying.

Gavin struggled to both hang on to Samantha while attempting to not be crushed in her grip, looked at Scott as he spoke.

"They went with the bad man with the gun," Gavin replied as he wiped away tears of his own with the palm of his hand.

"The what?" Scott asked in shock.

"The man with the gun took them with him," Gavin added. "Took them in his truck."

"Is this true?" Scott asked but seeing how upset Samantha was, he realized he didn't actually need an answer. He knew Samantha was crying for a reason and Gavin wouldn't make something like this up. It was stranger than fiction and while Gavin had a wild imagination, this wasn't something he could have made up. Gavin had no way of knowing Jack had a gun.

In that moment, Scott heard his cordless phone ring and reached to his belt to find the phone wasn't there. The phone rang again giving Scott a hint to its location. He glanced around on the third ring and saw it on the ground near the edge of the tree line. He must have dropped it when he ran after Bradley. He scooped it up and answered the call.

"Jack!" he screamed into the phone.

"What?" he heard the voice say in response.

"Jack?" Scott repeated. He had assumed Jack would be calling to demand something. A ransom? Something! What could he possibly want, wondered Scott?

"Scott?" Reverend Masterson said. "Scott, are you okay? What's going on?"

"I don't know," Scott blurted as he watched Samantha getting to her feet while trying to get herself under control. "I have no fuckin' idea, okay!"

He watched a trembling Samantha climb the back

stoop and take Gavin inside.

"Scott, tell me what's happening," Reverend Masterson demanded.

"Can you get over here?" Scott asked. "I need your help."

"I'll be right there," Reverend Masterson replied. He knew Scott normally didn't ask him for anything. "I'm coming right away," he said as he ended the call without any of the usual formalities.

Scott glanced back at the thick woods behind his house. *Bradley is gone*, he thought as he looked at the sock, still in his hand. Where the fuck had he gone? And since when did Jack Whitefeather abduct children? A feeling of helplessness washed over Scott as he looked around an empty back yard that was normally full of life. He looked at the sock and remembered he had just asked the righteous Reverend Masterson for help.

"God help me," he exclaimed, a comment that normally he would have found amusing, since he was an atheist. But in that moment, the comment felt fitting for if there was a God, Scott would need him right now. He would need him desperately.

Chapter 20
What Do We Do Now?

Burke stood next to Jin's parked SUV on Ocean's Edge Road. Facing the vehicle, the glare of the sun reflected off the windows. He looked back at his own reflection and that of the trees behind him. He cupped his hands around his face trying to cut the glare in order to get a better look inside the vehicle. The doors were locked. Burke pulled his cell phone and tried calling Jin once more, hoping that perhaps he would hear the cell phone ring amongst the clutter of maps, coolers and various stuff scattered inside the vehicle. Or that perhaps Jin would have found his stupid cell phone by now and would answer his call. *Unless Jin is actually ignoring my calls on purpose*, he thought.

Bradley staggered on, dragging his feet on the forest floor as he walked through the woods with one bare, bloody foot. The other battered foot was clad in a filthy sock that now had holes in it, both shoes gone long ago. He occasionally shuffled his feet as he walked; his head and shoulders slouched forward, he dragged dead leaves, bits and pieces of green plants as they caught on his feet. He walked on unaware of any of these things. He walked past a cell phone that lay on the ground, as it rang just as the battery icon flashed red. He walked past it, ignoring it

173

completely. The screen on the cell phone went black as the battery died.

A large deformed rat burst from the brush and stopped a few feet away from Bradley. The rat stood on its hind legs and sniffed at the air, before running off as fast as it had appeared. It left behind Bradley, who hadn't acknowledged it and continued on his slow but steady shamble through the forest. The only thought left on his mind was the task of getting to his destination.

Burke swore under his breath. He needed to talk to Jin but had no way of reaching him. As he peered inside the SUV again, he noticed a large, opened map of Oakwood Island spread out on the passenger seat. It had a large red circle drawn in an area that was a short hike from where he stood. He had no way of knowing for sure, but his instincts told him that Jin had left the map there for him to see.

There also seemed to be clutter under the maps, but Burke couldn't make out what that was. He did see Ziploc bags and other things. In the back seat were Jin's hiking boots so Burke assumed he would be wearing his running shoes, perhaps. This was strange as Jin was not the type to go on a trek without the proper foot gear. There was an open backpack which seemed to contain all the folders Jin had been studying. In the very back of the SUV sat a pair of large red plastic gas cans.

The sound of traffic caught his ear. He stopped to watch a lady drive past him. He waited until he saw the vehicle disappear around the next bend in the road. Turning his back to the SUV and leaning against it, he pondered his next move. Out of habit, he reached for his cigarettes and Zippo with the intention of lighting up, but soon remembered he was leaning against a car which contained plastic canisters of gasoline and changed his mind. He could wait for a cigarette, he thought, as he watched another small car being driven by an old man drive past. He could wait a little bit, he confessed to himself, but not for too long.

Looking down at his feet and back into the SUV, he used his deductive reasoning skills and assessed that the hiking boots were probably a size 8. He looked down at his feet which wore a size 10 battered pair of dress shoes and sighed. He took his large plastic framed glasses off and began cleaning them with the hem of his jacket while he wondered what to do next.

Chapter 21
Guiding Hands

"**N**o, Lily," Patrick said. He sat in the old truck between his twin sister Lily and Jack, the man who smelled like campfire.

Jack glanced at the twins as he drove, wondering what Patrick knew about his sister and her abilities. The kids had remained quiet until now. Why was he scolding his sister? Jack clutched the steering wheel with both hands as he drove a little faster than he normally would have. He hoped the police would be on the other side of the island, perhaps busied with something mundane while he worked to rid the island of an evil that had taken lives for decades. He glanced at the shotgun laying across the dashboard. A few times he had to hold it so it wouldn't slide when negotiating turns a little too fast.

Lily sat quietly, staring at her bald doll. "My doll's dead," Lily muttered as she bent the dolls limbs into positions no human could possibly attain. "Dead like my Mommy," Lily added.

"Was that dead lady in the hospital really our Mommy?" Patrick inquired as he adjusted his large sunglasses. He cocked his head to the side, listening for a response.

"What have they told you about that woman?" Jack asked, wondering just how much of this the four-year-olds would understand. They were both abnormally intelligent which made Jack wonder why they had been so willing to come with him. *Had they not been taught the dangers of strangers*, he thought, not realizing the irony in his thinking.

"Nothing," Lily replied as she stared at her doll.

"Was she our Mommy?" Patrick repeated his previous question, still wanting an answer.

"Yes," Jack replied. "She was."

"Why was she in the hospital?" Patrick asked.

"She was sick," Jack replied. "Very sick."

"Is Lily going to be sick like her too?" Patrick asked. "Is that why you're taking us there?"

Jack glanced at Patrick, mystified with how much he seemed to know. Jack slowed his truck as he drove past a familiar sedan and an SUV parked on the side of Ocean's Edge Road. Both vehicles looked empty of any occupants as he drove past, glancing in his rear view mirror to be sure. Jack put a hand on the shotgun to keep it from sliding as he went around a bend in the road. He pondered how to answer the boy's question. After rounding the bend, he saw a large upright figure emerge from the tree line, the thing covered in hair with long fangs and pointed ears. The familiar creature pounced into the road faster than Jack could react as he took his foot off the gas pedal, intending on stepping on the brakes but not having the time to do so. The snarling hairy beast stopped in the middle of the road, poised and ready to attack.

"No, Lily," Patrick said firmly.

The hairy beast stopped and remained motionless in that moment as the old red Ford truck drove through what Jack knew had been an apparition only he could see. But how had the boy known about it? He wondered this as he watched a crow fly over the roof of his truck, and up over the trees in the direction they were heading, as if it already knew where he was going. The crow circled three times before swooping down and out of sight.

Not long after his arrival at the Cudmore household, Reverend Masterson was met by an upset and panic-driven Scott. Sure, Scott would sometimes get annoyed and impatient, but he'd never personally seen him truly mad before now.

Scott realized he was showing a side to his father-in-law that had been rarely if ever seen, but he couldn't help it. His worry and panic were mounting by the minute. He told the Reverend to go check on Samantha in the living room, as he made a call to the small police force of Oakwood Island.

The dispatcher, Sandy, picked up on the first ring. She spoke fast, "Oakwood Island Emergency Line."

"Sandy, it's Scott Cudmore. Jack Whitefeather took my twins in his truck. You need to send help, now!"

"Scott, wait, what? Jack? Who took the twins?"

"Yes, Jack Whitefeather!"

"Is this a joke? You know we don't like getting crank calls, Scott–"

He interrupted her before she could finish. His voice harsh and demanding.

"Sandy, I swear, if you don't send someone to help NOW, I will go find him myself, and I promise you I will not think twice about doing whatever I have to..."

Sandy's voice returned to the professional tone she had answered the call with.

"Tell me which direction he was headed, Scott."

"He headed north from my house. Sandy, please...these are my babies..." Scott's voice cracked again, and hot tears formed in his eyes.

"I'm sending two cars now, Scott. Hang tight. If you see them again, call me back right away."

Scott didn't wait to hear anything else. He hung up the phone and looked out the window. As he spotted the forest in the back yard, he realized that he had completely forgotten to mention Bradley and how his teenage ward had wandered off. Only now did he remember the boy walking off into the woods on his own. Since the porcupine incident, the boy had expressed his fear of going into the woods. He had been scared to come across another such creature and would never have ventured off in the forest, especially not alone. Bradley was old enough to know better, unlike the twins who were practically babies still, thought Scott.

Scott walked back to the living room, where he saw that his father-in-law was trying to calm Samantha.

"I should have paid more attention to them. I should have tried to stop him." Her sobs seeped through each word. Her grandfather spoke in a soft and reassuring voice to help her calm down. Under normal circumstances, Scott would have been able to pacify the situation without issue, but in his agitated state that ability had vanished, replaced by a feeling of mounting frustration. Samantha, a bit calmer, turned her attention to Gavin, making sure he was all right.

As soon as his father in law saw Scott in the foyer area, he exited the living room and joined him. Scott kicked off his loafers and grabbed his running shoes. He spoke in haste to his father in law as he started putting on one of his sneakers.

"Peter, Colin and Clay, will have to stay at their friend's place until Miriam can go get them." Scott said to Reverend Masterson without waiting for a reply. Done putting on his second sneaker, he walked quickly to the kitchen area again. The Reverend followed him down the hall, but not too close.

"Bradley will come back home when he's good and ready. I don't have time to go chasing after him with the twins gone." Scott caught himself choking up at the mention of the twins. He needed to focus on what he had to do now and keep his emotions out of it. He cleared his throat as he grabbed his cell and car keys off the kitchen counter and exited via the patio door.

"Where are you going?" Reverend Masterson asked.

"To look for the twins," Scott replied.

"Where?" the Reverend asked.

"I don't fucking know," Scott blurted in a harsh tone as he got into the old minivan, slamming the door. He turned the key and heard a clicking sound. A feeling of hopelessness washed over him as he tried to start the van a second time and heard nothing but a clicking noise again coming from under the hood. With a quick glance in the rearview mirror, he knew the back door hadn't been shut properly and the dome light had drained the battery yet again. Scott wasn't very knowledgeable when it came to motor vehicles, but this wasn't the first time one of the kids didn't close the back door properly. He scrambled out of his seat, climbed in the back of the van, shut the door hard and got back into the driver's seat. He gripped the steering wheel, leaned his head against it and prayed for the first time in his life, asking a God he didn't really believe in for help to save his children.

Scott would never understand the truth behind what happened next. It wasn't the actions of God that came to Scott's aid in that moment, but the love of a mother. Even if she had never really known them in life, her spirit would stop at no end to protect them now.

The shimmering spirit of Norah Jenkins with her multicolored aura appeared before the van, unseen by Scott. She now knew the man before her was the reason her children knew love. Even if Lily had the same evil in her that had cursed her own sister and her family for generations, this man showed the child love. Because of this man, her twins had a family to care for them when she couldn't.

The spirit of Norah reached a glimmering hand forward and laid it on the hood of the van as Scott prayed for help from a God he had never believed in but now in his hypocrisy, begged for help. Scott, with his head still on the steering wheel, reached down and turned the key once more in the hopes that perhaps there was a God and that he wouldn't have abandoned him in this hour of desperate need. The van's engine roared to life, surprising Scott as he sat upright in his seat, buckled his seatbelt and murmured his thanks to a God he still questioned deep down inside. Scott put the van in reverse and inched backward only to pause at the end of his driveway. The first place he knew he should go to was Jack's cabin in the woods, but the small Oakwood Island police force would likely be thinking the same thing. They would surely beat him there. At least he hoped they would.

Scott didn't know why, but he turned left. Driving off in a hurry without any idea where you were going was something he would normally have said was stupid. But in the heat of the moment, he had to do something and sitting still while others looked for his kids wasn't it.

Jack was nearing his destination. There was a dirt road, if it could be called a road, coming up on this part of the island. He would drive up this beaten path as far as he could and walk the rest of the way from there. He'd carry the children if he had to. This needed to be done, he kept repeating to himself, trying to shut out the doubts that came to him more and more as he drove on. He felt sick, as if he might vomit at the thought of killing children, but he didn't know any other way. Edwina Quartley was expected to never regain consciousness. Ben Augustine would never walk normal again, if he could walk at all. Unless he did this, the new occupants of the old Ketchum house would pay the price, the same as the Ketchum's had. There was no doubt the evil had to end, but for the first time, he wished there was another way and that perhaps someone else would end it for him. For the first time in his life, he didn't want to be the one who had to save the people of Oakwood Island.

Without the help of the crow, Jack couldn't see the spirits that wandered Oakwood Island. He knew they were real as he spent most of his life watching them. However, without the help of his feathered friend, he had no way of seeing the shimmering spirit with the multicolored aura that stood in the middle of Ocean's Edge Road. Norah Jenkins stood in the path of the oncoming truck, raised her hands before her, palms out and locked eyes on the man who had taken her children. The old truck drove through her spirit without pause. But when it did, the truck began leaving a small trickle of gasoline as one of the old patches on the gas tank had suddenly failed and sprung a leak. Soon the trickle would intensify, becoming a small stream, leaving a wet trail of fuel on the road behind it.

The faster Scott drove his minivan, the more convinced he became that he was heading in the right direction. He had no idea why he felt this way, but the feeling edged him on. His heart raced as he sped down Ocean's Edge Road. He had no idea what Jack had in mind for a pair of innocent children, but he knew whatever it was, he wouldn't let it happen.

Sitting next to Scott in the minivan was the spirit of Norah Jenkins, her multicolored aura shimmering brightly as she lay a hand on the dash of the van. She knew where Scott needed to go even if he didn't and she would make sure he would get there. Her eyes sparkled bright colors as she guided Scott's hands and the van towards her biological children, the twins that Scott loved as much as if they were his very own. She knew that working together was the only way they could save the twins from certain death.

Her soul, now freed from the curse in the afterlife, knew there was another important reason to stop Jack's plan. She saw how the curse had started decades before. Ending it would also mean fulfilling a destiny that would bring even more decay and death to the island. She knew that the one dark spirit that was at the core of the curse could not have her twin's souls. In the afterlife, protecting her children had become her only mission.

Jack's old 1950's faded red truck sat on the side of

Ocean's Edge Road with a small puddle of gasoline under it, a shotgun still laying across the dash and the keys still in the ignition.

Winded and sweating heavily, Jack walked along Ocean's Edge Road with a child in each arm. His truck had run out of fuel a quarter mile from his destination. With no time to waste, he'd scooped up the children and walked to get to the dirt covered Dead Man's Road that led to the cliffs. Jack felt as if his age was finally catching up to him as he struggled with the weight of the children, but he pressed on. The pain in his chest, not quite as strong as before had returned. The stress of it all bearing down on him as he walked, he asked his ancestors for the strength to carry this through but felt they were not listening. Perhaps killing children, even if they were evil was something they wouldn't help him with. He knew his ancestors would have no part in this, nor would they help him.

"Almost there," Patrick said as Jack turned off the road and onto the beaten path.

How does the boy know this? Jack wondered. And if he knew that, then did he know what fate waited for them on the small clearing on the edge of the cliff?

Chapter 22
A Walk in the Woods

Burke stopped to look at his phone and up at the trees. The wind made the leaves overhead shake and bend the smaller branches just a bit. Not being any kind of outdoorsman, he had zero idea of what he was doing out in the woods. It had taken four tries until he'd managed to take a good enough picture of the map in the SUV through the glass. Since he recalled Jin mentioning a compass app on his phone to help navigate, Burke had discovered that he too had such an app on his cell phone. So in getting his bearings as best as he could, he had headed off into an awkward hike. He soon realized his shoes were obviously not made for this type of terrain. He also noticed that the compass app wasn't very reliable. When he went to the image of the map and back to the compass, North had changed direction.

Burke couldn't help but feel the irony of his thinking as he walked in the dense forest, towards what he thought was the area Jin had marked on the map in his SUV. What struck Burke as ironic was how he had obsessed about solving what had killed so many people, including Officer Ryan McGregor, the Stuarts and the Watsons. He would have never assumed those deaths would have been linked to Maggie's abduction until Jin came along. He had found himself thinking about Jin Hong's obsession with the fungus found on Oakwood Island. The same fungus Jin insisted shouldn't be able to survive a winter here on this island, let alone thrive as he had insisted it did.

Jin's suggestions that all this had to do with the fungus or spores or whatever the hell he called that crap was ridiculous. He might as well have suggested Big Foot was real and that he was a space alien, that's how ridiculous all this was. Or at least that was Burke's initial thinking. He was thinking about this as he debated how to tell Jin what coroner Harold Randolf had said about exhuming bodies to look for evidence of spores. Burke found himself with a better understanding of why Randolf gave him those weird looks whenever he obsessed over the brutal killings as he argued that some type of werewolf might be behind it all. Now he knew why Randolf thought he was crazy.

Stupid cell phone, Burke thought as he looked up and noticed some branches snapped and bent downwards. He had seen that earlier on his walk and had assumed it was done by a moose. There were a lot of moose on Oakwood Island, but he assumed he might have seen tracks or something. Shouldn't he have? A moose is a heavy animal and so should leave tracks in what was pretty soft ground. When he examined the branches closely, he came to realize that they were about the same height as the last ones he saw; around shoulder height, perfectly within reach of someone as they walked past, perhaps wanting to leave a trail to find the location again. Were these a simple form of trail markers? He tried to recall if Jin had mentioned this when they spoke last, but didn't think he had.

Burke adjusted his glasses and looked at the compass app which was back to pointing at what he had previously assumed was the correct North. He decided the snapped and bent branches were roughly in the direction he was going and felt they were there for a reason. He trusted them just a smidge more than the technology on his phone and so he continued to follow them.

Burke continued his hike as best he could. He had slipped, stumbled and staggered during much of his hike because of the smooth soles of his worn dress shoes. As he walked, he checked the compass app on his phone, still uncertain if it would help him or fail him. Trying to point the cell in various directions to get a proper reading, he didn't see the large mossy rock that the tip of his dress shoe hit hard. Tumbling over the large rock, his body went down fast. He landed face down on the mossy forest floor, bits and pieces of branches and leaves stuck on his scraped hands which he had put out to try to avoid the fall.

Burke cursed at himself for not having the proper footwear for a hike in the woods as he lifted himself up on hands and knees and got into a kneeling position. He checked the most important thing on his person, his package of Peter Jackson menthol cigarettes. The pack seemed a bit crushed, so he pulled it out to examine the contents. The pack, which only contained eight cigarettes in total, now had three broken, two slightly bent and three that survived unscathed. He sighed as he took one of the broken ones, cast aside the broken tip and placed the balance of it in his mouth. He patted his pockets, found his Zippo and lit the short cigarette. He inhaled the smoke deeply, coughed and exhaled in between more coughs. He examined himself, saw how dirty he was and so didn't really mind the damp feeling he was getting beneath his knees as he knelt on the ground. He removed his glasses and decided he had no clean bit of shirt or jacket to clean them with and so put them back on. Large spots of drying mud spatter and dirt speckled his eyesight through the large lenses.

While taking another drag of his short cigarette, he realized that he must have dropped his cell phone when he fell as he had held it when he had gone down. Burke saw the phone on the ground, a few feet before him. He got to his feet, dusted himself off some as he retrieved his cell phone that lay on the damp moss. When he retrieved his phone, he noticed another phone on the ground only a few feet from his.

He pocketed his cell phone and picked up the other one, all while wondering if this was Jin Hong's lost cell phone. After a few tries to activate it, he realized the battery had to have died. He tried to recall what Jin's phone looked like but couldn't remember any details about it. Although, who else had been trampling about these woods recently? *It has to be Jin's*, he thought. The thought of swapping batteries occurred to him, to see if the phone really was Jin's, but his was an older model and this one was newer. He couldn't even tell how to open the damned thing, so that was out of the question.

He puffed at his cigarette, which was already mostly gone as he looked about. Burke froze as he saw a weird shape in a tree nearby. Walking forward a few steps, he saw in front of him, dangling from a tree branch a large decomposing animal that looked like what had been a rabbit. Suspended from what appeared to be its mouth, the dead rabbit dangled, its stomach completely burst open with a few small pieces of entrails dangling from the gaping hole.

"Lord Almighty," Burke uttered. "What the fuck is that?"

Burke looked at the cell phone in his hand, the one he

had just found and knew right away that this was what Jin must have been referring to. He dropped his cigarette and stepped on it until he was satisfied he had properly extinguished it. Jin must have found this, he thought. That's why he panicked. The rabbit hung in the tree like the zombie ants of the Peruvian Amazon. He remembered Jin speaking of ants only and nothing else. Nothing of this size, he thought.

That's when he saw movement in the forest up ahead. Something had moved, he was sure of it. He watched carefully until he saw it again.

"Jin!" he shouted as he marched forward, not daring a run in his poor choice of shoes. He walked on until he saw a young man he had never seen before, who was in the middle of climbing a large maple tree. Burke noticed the boy had one bare, bloody foot, while the other wore a filthy, torn sock. The teenage boy looked in shambles as he scrambled up the tree with ease, leaving bloody prints wherever he touched the tree trunk. The boy turned his head and Burke saw a blank expression on his face. From this distance it was hard to discern, but it seemed that the boy showed no strain in his efforts to climb this tall tree. The boy looked up at a tree branch which was out of reach. Shifting his position on the tree, he launched himself at the branch, hands dangling at his sides as he did so. Burke looked in shock at the impossible feat as he watched the boy clutch the branch in his mouth as his body swayed from the exertion.

Burke stood dumbfounded as he watched the boy struggle to get a better hold while his arms merely dangled at his sides. As the swaying stopped, the boy's discolored skin stretched out, gradually separating into sections of flesh, until the boy's stomach burst open. The t-shirt he had been wearing was forced up by the outpouring of

189

his blackened entrails and what looked like pollen which floated on the gentle breeze in the wooded area.

"What the fuck?" Burke muttered, wondering if he had finally lost his mind or if he was really seeing this. He staggered back a few steps in horror of what he had just witnessed. Finally, he understood why Jin was so worried about the spread of this mutated strain of zombie fungus as he watched some of the bits that had just come out of the boy's stomach float towards him.

Burke tugged and pulled at his shirt to cover his nose and mouth as he saw more of the particles floating in the air around him. Stepping back, he saw another body dangling from a tree branch on his right. A mature woman by the look of it hung the same way as the teenage boy did. Her stomach had been opened in the same way, with putrid pus and some entrails hanging from the opening. The rotting flesh of her face was distorted by the pull of gravity and she was not recognizable. Her long black hair was matted and only partially covered a visible gash she had suffered, which was now a bulbous mound of oozing pus. Not far behind her hung a bald man in a white coat in the same manner. Burke recognized him as the pharmacist who had recently questioned his sleeping pill refills. His flesh was not quite as stretched nor as decomposed yet, but he was very bloated. His hands hung large, almost like balloons. Two of the fingers had been gnawed off, more than likely by one of the critters he had seen in the forest. In the place of fingers there were now hanging sacs, which no doubt contained more of the spores, soon to be released in the air. Burke's mind raced.

How was this possible?

What could he do now?

Burke staggered backwards, tripped on a tree root and landed on his butt. When he did this, he got an idea of the scope of this discovery. On his left side, hanging from a tree was Grady, the idiot that had skipped out on Shelley at the restaurant. Where his eyes had been, there were two large formed sacs that started just above his nose and spread up and covered his entire forehead. One of them seemed to pulsate. It was no doubt ready to release its contents to spread itself. The kid's mouth was open, attached to the tree branch. Burke could see his cheeks, elongated, blue and full of swollen veins which hung loosely down and dripped a thick yellow pus.

Not far from him, Burke recognized Jin Hong, hanging from a tree like the ants he had been so fascinated with. Burke shook his head, not able to control his fear anymore. "No, no, no," he said aloud, quietly at first, then yelled, "Nooo!" He did not know what to do. Jin was the one that had the answers. Now here he was, hanging on a branch in the forest, his dead eyes staring out into nothing. Other than his opened stomach, his body was still intact, no sign of decomposition yet, but Burke knew it would come and he had no desire to see that.

He recognized the lady on the right of Jin too. He recalled seeing a picture of her in The Oakwood Chronicler. That was Peggy Martin. Had to be, he thought, as he watched in horror as the lower half of her body slowly detached from the upper half in a slow and slick motion, the sound of distended and rotting skin stretched too far, causing it to fall to the forest floor in a splatter. There, it exploded as it hit the ground, into a puddle of pus, blood, black entrails and rotten organs.

"Fuck me," Burke muttered as his mind swam with anxiety over what he had found. Turning, he felt the rush of vomit coming up. He spewed and spat. The mixed smell of his puke and the putrid bodies rotting in the heat bringing about another sudden bout of nausea and vomiting.

191

Blinking away tears, he wiped off his mouth and covered his face up to his cheeks again, to avoid breathing in any of the particles that was still highly visible in the air.

This can't be real, he thought. How could it be? Was he going crazy, like Randolf had implied when he last spoke to him?

Still seated on the mossy ground, Burke heard a rustling sound coming from behind him. He felt panic wash over him. As he spun around to look behind him, he heard a similar sound to his left. He spun to look there but saw nothing. Then as if out of nowhere, a large, weirdly deformed rat appeared before him. The rat raised itself on its hind legs and hissed at him like a cat. Burke scampered backwards as the rat's neck jutted forward and with its mouth open, it sprayed his face with a hot and sticky rancid liquid.

Burke scrambled to his feet, staggered until he found his footing and ran in the direction he had come. He ran a short distance before tripping on something and falling forward yet again, this time scraping his right elbow which took most of the impact.

He ignored the pain as he pulled off his jacket as well as his glasses and wiped at his face. The sticky spit felt like it irritated his skin as he wiped off as much as he could. Thank God his glasses had stopped that shit from getting into his eyes, he thought as he wiped it as best as he could. Hearing the shuffling sound coming from behind him, panic set in as he got to his feet and ran as fast as he could.

Chapter 23
The Return

Jack's hair fluttered in the wind under the rim of his hat, winds that had grown in strength as he limped up the beaten path. Each twin walked by his sides, each one of them holding him by the hand willingly. The pain in Jack's chest was back, although not as strong as before. Somehow, he knew that this was all stress related. He had come to realize this before, and now more than ever, as he marched towards what would be a life changing event for him. Once he had done this and saved the people of Oakwood Island from evil, he would never be able to return to any kind of normal life. Not this time. Nobody would understand why he, a man many loved, had felt it necessary to kill children. Nobody understood that these children were touched by an evil that simply wouldn't let them go. An evil that clung to their family and had been passed on generation after generation. The good people of Oakwood Island didn't know anything about curses and evil, nor would they believe him if he tried to explain it to them. Only a select few had knowledge of these things, and Jack was the only one with enough courage to face it.

He intended to sever the tie of evil to the Jenkins family once and for all. The children he needed to kill to do so were now leading him to the place where he had to do it. This confused Jack, as he had expected to have to drag them kicking and screaming to the clearing on the cliff. Instead, they clutched his hands in theirs and led him up the path. Patrick, walking on Jack's left side, led him by one hand with his other hand outstretched out of habit to make sure he wouldn't walk into anything. Lily on his right side, walked with determination as she clutched in her other hand what was left of a Barbie doll, a torso and leg.

"I'm gonna be like my Mommy," Lily said.

Jack wondered what the little girl meant. Was she referring to the evil that had held a grasp on her mother, like it had done to her grandmother as well? Was she referring to the evil that clung to her and had taken the lives of the Ketchum couple? Or was she referring to the fact that Norah was now dead. Was she referring to the fact that she, too, would soon be dead? *What do the children know and how do they know this?* Jack wondered.

The crow flew high overhead as they walked. It carried something in its claws, something oblong and white. Jack could feel it watching from above. He wondered what it saw. Was the spirit of Sparrow Whitefeather here with him? Would she guide him? Would she help him? A part of him regretted not ending it at the Cudmore house. It would have been much easier to bear, to end it quickly. Somehow, he knew that had he done this the evil would have continued. Unsure how it could with no twins to continue the lineage, he hadn't dared risk it. The crow that had guided him all of his life had shown him this place. It must have done so for a reason. Something deep inside him knew this was where the evil needed to be stopped. The bird swooped down using the winds to glide and Jack saw that the bird carried something in its beak as it disappeared over the trees that were now swaying in the wind. Somehow Jack knew the crow would be waiting for him at the clearing near the cliffs edge. Waiting where he believed it all started long ago.

As the twins led Jack into the windy clearing, he marveled at the sight before him. He had wandered much of Oakwood Island which meant he had been to this area before and remembered the clearing and the view of the old lighthouse off in the distance. Today was different though. The area he remembered did not look like how he found it today. He remembered the firm soil beneath the grassy area, as if just beneath it was packed soil and bedrock. He recalled the trees that surrounded the edge of the area but none had ever grown in the center of the small clearing.

What lay before him, just beyond the swaying trees was a grassless patch of dirt. Jack smelled the combination of sea air and fresh soil as if it had been recently exposed. He saw bugs and worms wriggling in the fresh earth, many burrowing themselves back into the ground. He and Lily watched as Patrick cocked his head, listening as the winds became stronger here, swaying the large trees behind them. Jack watched as a strong gust blew more dirt away from the clearing.

The crow flew low and dropped what it had been carrying in its beak. The object landed in the middle of the circle of dirt and then the crow landed on it. The bird cawed loudly as it stood on what Jack knew was his grandmother's bone dagger. The bird pecked at the bone and cawed repeatedly.

"We're here," Patrick said as he stopped before Jack.

Chapter 24
A Smoke and a Promise

Burke's addiction to tobacco had never been something he thought much about. He smoked. Deal with it. That's what he had told his wife, not long before she told him she wanted a divorce. That wasn't why she divorced him, but it was never something that she liked about him. A former smoker herself, she had given him a lot of slack when it came to his smoking. She had begged him to quit, not for her, but for his own health. She knew he smoked away his stress. The job, which was the main reason for his habit, was why she eventually did divorce him. Right now though, wheezing and his head spinning, he thought maybe she was right after all. Smoking may just end up killing him.

He had run as far and as fast as he could which turned out to be, not far at all. Pushing himself on the hike had left him wheezing for breath for most of the way there but especially on the run back. With the vehicles now in sight, he wheezed and struggled for breath. Looking back behind him, he figured those things that looked like giant rats on steroids hadn't followed him. At least he didn't think they had. The fire in his lungs felt like it was diminishing finally as he walked towards Ocean's Edge Road on legs that felt like rubber.

Once at the SUV, he turned his back to it, leaned against it and slumped down to the ground. He stretched his legs out and sat with his back against the vehicle. Out of habit, he pulled the pack of cigarettes from his breast pocket. The pack was damp with the same perspiration that had soaked his shirt through and through. Opening the pack, he saw every single cigarette was partially crushed from the many tumbles and stumbles due to his trek in the woods in bad footwear. He blamed the bad footwear, although poor health had more to do with it. He struggled to admit the second part, but there was no kidding himself. He pulled the most intact piece of cigarette from the box and put it between his lips. He crushed the box and tossed it on the ground. He patted his pockets until he found his Zippo. He lit the piece of cigarette which struggled to burn as it was dampened with perspiration. Burke launched into a coughing fit that had the world around him spinning out of control. He gasped for breath as the world dimmed for a moment as he came incredibly close to passing out. He flicked the cigarette onto the asphalt of Ocean's Edge Road as he hocked up phlegm and spat.

"If I live through this, I need to quit smoking," Burke mumbled as he struggled to his feet. His legs still felt weak but at least the urge to vomit and faint was less intense now. His head spun a bit at first when he got on his feet, but he steadied himself. He looked at the Zippo in his hand and at the gas cans in the back of the SUV and understood what Jin had in mind. The doors were locked. He went to his car, retrieved the tire iron which he found under a box of old case files in the back seat.

Still in a bit of a daze from his exertions, he found himself bashing in the back window of the SUV with the tire iron. The SUV's alarm was deafening. With no keys to turn it off, he cursed at his luck. Had he been thinking clearer, he would have remembered the alarm. He went to the SUV's driver side door, bashed in that window, reached in and felt for the hood latch. Once he popped the hood, he disconnected the SUV's battery by prying off one of the terminals using the tire iron, however the deafening alarm kept blaring. *Damned thing has a small back up battery somewhere*, thought Burke.

He hopped into the SUV and felt around until he found the fuse panel and began randomly plucking out fuses until the alarm finally died, but the ringing in his ears continued. He cast a glance towards the woods, worried the monster rat creatures might have heard the noise and come looking, but nothing stirred. Burke walked behind the SUV, tire iron clutched firmly in his right hand, as if he expected to be attacked by something. Another glance up and down the road showed nothing either, so he felt he was good to keep going.

He sighed in relief and reached into the vehicle to take out the two gas canisters. He set them on the ground next to him, tucked the tire iron into his belt like they did with swords in the movies, and patted his breast pocket looking for cigarettes that were no longer there.

Scanning the ground, he saw his recently discarded cigarette and retrieved it. He lit the piece and puffed away the last little bit of it while he looked at the gas canisters before him. He glanced at his cigarette, felt the Zippo in his pants pocket and marveled at his own stupidity. Gas canisters which had been locked in a hot vehicle for hours sat next to him while he lit a cigarette, he thought. He was the guy who made jokes about these dumb people. He exhaled smoke as he flung the cigarette behind him onto Ocean's Edge Road again where he had just retrieved it. *I've really lost it*, he thought, *if I've ever really had it at all*, he chuckled.

He picked up the gas canisters, strapped on Jin's backpack and marched off into the forest in the same direction he had come. Jin was right. This had to be done.

Chapter 25
Off the Beaten Path

Scott's stomach tightened into an acidic ball as he glanced down at the minivan's gas gauge and saw he was low on fuel. If he was headed in the wrong direction, he might regret his decision to head out looking for the kids without thinking it through. Searching for them was devastating enough but imagining being broken down on the side of the road after running out of gas, helpless while Jack Whitefeather did God knows what to them, would be much worse. This thought weighed heavily on him since he drove past a car and an SUV broken down on the roadside. He had wanted to stop and ask if they had seen Jack's truck, but the man was under the hood, the SUV's alarm was blaring, and Scott simply didn't feel he had time for any of that.

He tried to breathe and focus but panic always caught up to him. His cell phone hadn't rung since he yelled at his wife not to call him unless she had news and he would do the same. He didn't have time to talk. He needed to find his children. They were his responsibility and he couldn't live with himself if he let them down when they needed him most. Just when the stress of it all felt like it was getting to be too much, he saw Jack's truck on the side of Ocean's Edge Road.

His minivan screeched to a halt behind the truck leaving skid marks as he came to an abrupt stop. Scott got out in a panic and ran to the truck. Looking inside, he saw an empty seat where he had hoped to find his kids. In a way he was glad to find it empty, it was certainly better than finding them injured, or worse. Looking inside the truck he saw the shotgun on the dash, the keys in the ignition and no blood. Maybe Jack hadn't hurt them yet. Maybe he hadn't done anything to them. He glanced around, in the ditch, at the edge of the forest by the road and saw no sign of them. Panic started to rise again, from deep in his abdomen, rising up to his throat, where he could feel the pressure mounting. He stopped, took a deep breath and reminded himself that the shotgun was still in the truck. That was a good sign. With that, Scott felt a sudden sense of calm wash over him. Unsure why, he felt abnormally calm. The thought that Lily and Patrick might not have been harmed yet was the only thing on his mind.

The multicolored aura surrounding the spirit of Norah Jenkins glowed bright as she laid her hand on Scott Cudmore's back, even if he didn't feel her do it. He had been standing next to Jack Whitefeather's truck, in a state of panic and that wouldn't help the children any. Norah had no idea why she had such influence on people and things in this state, but she did. Perhaps it was having been touched by evil while alive that allowed her spirit to do these things? She did not know, nor did she care. All she wanted was for Scott to calm himself and find the children before harm came to them. She knew time was running out.

Scott saw what he was looking for. A few meters from

the truck laid the plastic arm of a Barbie doll on the edge of the asphalt. They had walked from there. It was obvious to him now where Jack was headed with the kids.

Scott called Sandy at the Oakwood Island Police Department.

"Scott? Where are you?" Sandy demanded.

"I'm past the bend on Ocean's Edge Road, approaching Dead Man's Cliff. I found Jack's truck abandoned by the footpath leading up to the lookout."

"I'm sending someone to you, Scott. Hang on," Sandy replied.

"I'm going up by Dead Man's Road."

Scott ended the call without waiting for Sandy to tell him not to do anything stupid. He knew she would have told him that. When your children are at risk, doing something stupid is sometimes all you can do. Scott ran back to his minivan, stopped and then ran back to Jack's truck. He grabbed the shotgun from the dash and brought it with him. Not long after hitting the road again, he found himself convinced that he needed to stop at the first beaten path he came upon off of Dead Man's Road. There he saw recent tracks in the dirt path. One pair was large, with smaller sized prints on either side of the larger ones. Scott drove up the dirt road as fast as he could. He hoped he wasn't too late.

Jack Whitefeather knew there was no turning back now. There was something dark and sinister at play, and it had been for a long, long time. Something evil had a hold on these children. Having watched the wind strip dirt away from the clearing, Jack came closer to the cleared off area near the cliff. He looked at the bone that had been sharpened into a dagger. He wondered if his grandmother had kept the dagger all those years for this very moment. He knew something wanted this done, and maybe Sparrow had foreseen it. Perhaps the evil was tired of playing with children. Perhaps it wanted to be released from the bond as much as Jack wanted to release it. But how could he not do it?

He closed his eyes and pictured Edwin Quartley as he'd seen her on his last visit, in her hospital bed, comatose. He pictured Ben Augustine in his wheelchair, grimacing from pain that he might have to live with forever. There were many more that had fallen victim to the curse through many generations. If Lily could injure and kill so many before she turned five, Jack imagined that she would do much more harm than any who had come before her. Other Jenkins twins had had guardians who prevented them from harming people, but Lily and Patrick had no such guardians. Also blind from birth, Patrick would never be able to care for his twin sister like Norah had for her twin sister Amy.

The crow's cawing startled Jack from his deep thoughts as he saw Lily standing by the cliff's edge. She was looking down at the rocks as she clutched a doll's torso, which was all that was left of her doll. Patrick stood next to Jack as if waiting. He kept his head slightly tilted back as he listened to the wind shake the tree leaves all around them. The lighthouse stood tall in the distance.

Jack took Patrick's hand and led him to the patch of dirt before him, where the grass simply would not grow. Jack bent at the waist, picking up the sharpened bone and examined the ground before him. The wind had removed the topsoil, exposing the dirt below it, but he hadn't noticed that it was a perfect circle. In the exposed dirt he saw more rib bones, the bones of a hand and the edge of a skull protruding from the exposed thin layer of soil. These were human bones.

Jack felt a sudden shooting pain coursing through his left arm and into his chest as he looked at the sharpened bone in his hand and then at the blind boy next to him. Lily now stood on the inside of the circle of freshly overturned soil. She looked at Jack with an intensity that he recognized from earlier in the truck. The crow cawed twice.

The multicolored aura of Norah Jenkins glowed strong, casting a multitude of bright shimmering rays across the clearing in all directions as she laid a hand on Jack Whitefeather's back. His stress levels increased dramatically as he struggled with the idea of murdering these children. The crow cawed again.

In his mind's eye, Jack saw a vision of the Cudmore house as it burned. Screams were coming from the house as a large fire consumed it. From the flames, unharmed exited Lily and Patrick, walking hand in hand. Lily was smiling.

Jack felt the pain in his chest intensify. This was it. He was having a heart attack, he thought. He staggered forward, reaching out, grasping Lily by her shoulder as he raised the pointed bone overhead. He knew what he had to do. There was no doubt he needed to do this, in order to save the island for generations to come.

"Please forgive me," he said aloud to the spirits of Oakwood Island. It was now or never.

Jack heard a loud gunshot from behind him as he felt the wind of the buckshot whoosh by, missing his head by very little. Jack staggered as the pain in his chest got the better of him. Even with the pain in his chest, he found himself suddenly worried that the children had been shot. The same children he had intended on killing. Lily stepped backwards as a sly grin appeared on her face. Patrick covered his ears to protect them from the sudden loud noise that had startled the blind boy. Jack looked at the sharpened bone in his hand and then at a frightened Patrick.

Behind Jack, at the edge of the clearing, a teary-eyed Scott struggled clumsily with the shotgun. He was pumping it to reload and jammed a shell casing in the ejector port in the process.

"Jack...no!" Scott muttered as he tried to free the jammed shell casing.

"Please forgive me," Jack said to the children as he clutched his chest and struggled to stand.

For a brief moment, he realized that there was a chance he would survive his heart attack and found he no longer wanted to. Although he knew he had to end the curse, he could not bring himself to do it in the way his grandmother had instructed him. He realized he could end it all himself, and without causing more pain and evil to affect these children, and so many more. He decided he didn't want the curse to survive for even one more day, and because of this he couldn't chance that he would survive either. He saw no other option. *It is my time to die*, he thought. It was time to let the people of Oakwood Island fend for themselves. Evil be damned, he simply couldn't murder children.

He turned the pointed end of the bone to his chest and let himself fall forward, impaling himself on the sharpened bone. The bone pierced his chest and protruded from his back. Jack felt the squeezing in his chest subside as the pain from the sharpened bone replaced it. Rolling to his side, blood trickling from the corner of his mouth, Jack watched Lily walk past him and run towards Scott. Jack heard the crow caw as his vision blurred.

Drifting off into what felt like a slumber he would not awaken from, Jack blinked twice, unsure of how to feel about what he was seeing. The last thing he saw before taking his last earthly breath was Lily smiling up at Scott Cudmore. The last thing he heard brought peace to his soul. Jack could feel his grandmother's presence stronger than ever.

"Thank you, grandson. Thank you for ridding the children of the curse, once and for all." Jack felt his grandmother's soft touch on his forehead just as everything went dark.

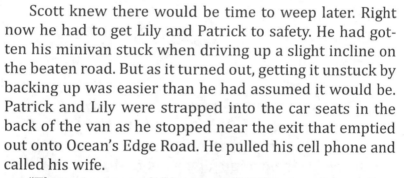

Scott knew there would be time to weep later. Right now he had to get Lily and Patrick to safety. He had gotten his minivan stuck when driving up a slight incline on the beaten road. But as it turned out, getting it unstuck by backing up was easier than he had assumed it would be. Patrick and Lily were strapped into the car seats in the back of the van as he stopped near the exit that emptied out onto Ocean's Edge Road. He pulled his cell phone and called his wife.

"The twins are safe," he blurted. "They're with me."

He heard his wife burst into sobs.

"Miriam?"

"Scott?" Reverend Masterson asked. "Is that you?"

"Yes," Scott replied. "Is Miriam okay?"

"She's upset, Scott. What did you say to her?"

"The twins," Scott repeated. "They're ok. They're with me," he added as he watched the children in the back seat. The pair sat quietly next to each other. Patrick smiled and Lily looked on at Scott. It was like he was seeing her for the first time. Something about her face was different. It took him a moment to realize that it was a look of peaceful contentment.

"Where's Jack Whitefeather?" Reverend Masterson asked.

"Dead," Scott replied. "Jack's dead."

"Thank God," the Reverend replied without realizing what he had said.

"Can you call Sandy at the police station and tell her I'm on Ocean's Edge Road and almost out of gas. Tell her I've got the twins, they're safe and that I'm bringing them back."

"Of course," Reverend Masterson replied. "God bless you, Scott."

"And tell Sandy Jack's dead," Scott added. "And tell Miriam we're coming home."

Blood pooled under Jack's now lifeless body on the freshly exposed soil. The blood flowed into the straight lines that darted away from his body in every direction. A pattern began emerging in the soil around the body. The shape of a pentagram appeared in the blood-soaked soil. Faint at first, billowing smoke started rising from the blood-filled lines that formed the pentagram in the soil. The black smoke soon gave way to flickering flames. The flames rose out of the ground in the lines of the pentagram, and as the winds grew in strength, the flames grew higher.

The crow cawed loud as it flew into the center of the circle and landed on the late Jack Whitefeather's shoulder. It cawed over and over, relentless as it called upon the many it called its brethren. The trees surrounding the clearing began filling with crows. One by one, they arrived, then in pairs and eventually in large flocks; they flew in from all directions and filled the trees surrounding the flaming pentagram. The crow in the center of the pentagram spread its wings wide, flapping them hard, strong wings fanning the flames until they grew and Jack's dead body caught fire. The crow hovered in the center of the flaming circle for a moment, its beady eyes looking at the murder that had filled every branch of the trees covering the area. The black eyes of the bird turned to a greyish white as it blinked, and the murder of crows took flight and began flying in swarms around the single crow.

They circled over and over as more crows joined in the ceremonial flight. Their combined black bodies created a pulsating motion, swooping around and around, closing in tighter and closer to the crow in the center. A sudden force exploded from the middle of the burning circle making all the birds fly away in random directions. Among the flames stood the naked body of a brown-skinned woman who stood in the circle of fire. The bones in the circle of exposed earth were gone, as was the one that Jack had impaled himself with.

The woman smiled. She bent down and using her long fingernails she scooped out Jack Whitefeather's eyes. Standing over his burning body which lay in the blood-soaked dirt, she laughed.

"Be my eyes, my old friend," she said mockingly, laughing before she swallowed his eyes whole.

Not far from the cliff, near the clearing where the body of Jack Whitefeather lay burning before a naked, brown-skinned woman, a wooden crate floated to the surface of the sea. Near that, a large sealed bottle floated to the surface in turn. A gnarled wooden staff appeared on the water's surface next to a few smaller little bottles and vials. All of which began a slow but steady drift towards the shore of Oakwood Island.

Parked on the side of Ocean' Edge Road Scott adjusted his rear view mirror so he could watch the children as they waited for the police to arrive. He wiped away a tear as he saw Patrick smiling, reached out patting the seat next to him until he found what he wanted. Patrick took Lily's hand in his and smiled. They sat, both of them quiet, in the back seat until Lily broke the silence.

"My dolly's broken," Lily said, a sad expression on her face as she examined the remnants of her Barbie doll.

"We'll get you a new one," Scott replied who struggled to keep his voice from showing emotion. "We'll get you a new one soon."

Chapter 26
Jin Was Right

Burke's legs felt like cement. His feet throbbed, his calves hurt and his back ached. All that plus his head throbbed from what he assumed was dehydration. He didn't remember the last time he pushed his body this much. It had to have been during his old police academy days, back when he ran for fun. Back when he actually enjoyed exercising. Now as a much older man, he found himself exhausted to the point where he felt he might collapse, and yet he still craved a cigarette more than anything. *I'm definitely crazy*, he thought as he pulled off the backpack, setting it on the ground near a pile of black goop. The strange part was that there were no flies on or around it. He'd seen enough dead things in his career as a detective to know there should be flies and bugs buzzing around it. He looked up at the trees and figured the black goo must have come from Grady.

"Grady, you little shit," he muttered. "Even you didn't deserve this."

He opened a gas canister and poured a small amount on the backpack watching it soak into the papers and fabric. Not only was Jin right about this, he was also right about not letting this get into the wrong hands. That simply couldn't happen. Burke proceeded to make a trail in the directions where the other bodies hung in the trees. He stood for a moment and watched the trees sway in the wind. Having assessed the wind's direction being in his favor, he backtracked making a trail with the rest of the gasoline in the first canister. Burke discarded the empty jug and fetched the second one. With this one he made a trail to where the rabbit hung in the tree. He assumed this was the farthest he had seen any of the evidence of the unexplainable mould before him. While in the process of making a line of fuel, he heard a rustling sound in the brush behind him.

Panic set in as he saw a large deformed rat emerging from the brush. It was the size of a raccoon. He set down the can and pulled the tire iron from his belt. Behind the large rat, he saw more movement of what looked like another of its kind, whatever it was. Burke fiddled with his large plastic framed glasses, unaware of the fate they had saved him from. The large raccoon-sized rat rose up on its hind quarters and sniffed at the air, its thick tail curled up behind it.

"Whatever the fuck you are, you smell the gas, don't you?" Burke said while clutching the tire iron like a weapon. While not taking his eyes off the creature, he took the remaining canister and continued pouring a line of fuel in front of the area where the bodies hung in the trees.

One of the deformed rats burst from the brush and ran past Burke, through the line of fuel he had just poured. A deafening, screeching sound coming from behind startled him. Burke turned and saw one of the rat things sitting on a tree branch above the dead rabbit. He turned and saw the first rat thing that had emerged from the brush now rush past him. He panicked and flung the tire iron at the rat and missed. The large rat continued towards the area where the bodies hung, completely bypassing Burke.

Burke frantically patted his pockets, found his Zippo, pulled it out and looked at it.

"Fuck it," he exclaimed as he lit the Zippo and tossed it into the fuel. There was a loud WHOOSH sound and the flames raced down the trail of gasoline he had poured. In mere moments, he stood watching flames as they consumed the dry forest debris, feeding a fire that grew by the second. Burke heard another screeching sound coming from the trees behind the fire line. One of the large rat things was on fire, flames spouting from its matted fur. He saw it scurry and climb a tree the way a cat tries to outrun pain.

"Burn, you fuck!" Burke said as he watched the wind spread the fire faster than he assumed it would. The wind blew the flames towards the dangling bodies, reaching them quickly, setting them ablaze along with the trees. Burke watched as Grady Foster's body fell from the tree as it burned. It hit the ground in a loud thump and splat as the body's liquefied insides spread out when it hit the forest floor. That was enough for the former detective. He had seen enough, he thought as he turned and began walking back the way he had come.

Chapter 27
The Oakwood Chronicler
July 26ᵗʰ

INVESTIGATORS CONFIRM
FOREST FIRE AS ARSON.
BY NICOLE BANFORD

On July 23ʳᵈ, local Oakwood Island volunteer fire-fighters responded to a forest fire off Ocean's Edge Road on the northern part of Oakwood Island. With the help of sudden hard rain that wasn't in the forecast, and the Bayview Fire Department, they managed to contain the blaze for a full day before the fire reached the edge of the cliffs and ran out of fuel. The only buildings consumed by the fire were on the property of Michael and Tracy Stuart, the former home of the late Robert and Nancy Stuart.

Later that day, former Bayview Detective George Burke, who was on sick leave and not on active duty, was arrested for setting the fire. What was believed to be a simple case of arson took a gruesome turn when the remains of seventeen people were discovered in the section of the burnt forest. Police are now saying that the fire was deliberately set in an attempt to destroy evidence of these grisly murders. Sources say the victims were gutted; their entrails left in piles near the bodies which had been dumped on the ground.

Local residents are now calling the former detective The Disemboweler. Formal charges of murder, arson, and tampering with evidence are expected to be filed later in the week. Burke is being held at the Daye Psychiatric Ward of the Oakwood Island Hospital for assessment.

James Hughes, police chief at the Oakwood Island police department has only released some of the names of the victims: Bradley Cornwell, age 15, Grady Foster, age 17, Tracy Stuart, age 32, Jin Hong, age 38, and Peggy Martin, age 67. The remaining victim's names will be released once relatives have been notified.

Nicole Banford is a staff reporter for The Oakwood Chronicler and can be reached at OakwoodChronicler@gmail.com

FAMOUS TWINS RETURNED HOME SAFE AND SOUND. BY TIMOTHY BANFORD

On July 23rd, while a fire was being set off at Ocean's Edge Road, Scott Cudmore searched frantically for his famous twin wards whom had been abducted by Oakwood Island resident Jack Whitefeather.

The reasons are still under investigation, but while another ward of the Cudmore household, Bradley Cornwell, was falling victim to the Disemboweler, Jack Whitefeather abducted foster twins Patrick and Lily Jones at gunpoint. Sources say the abduction took place while Scott Cudmore was off trying to find Bradley Cornwell whom had possibly been abducted minutes earlier by the Disemboweler. While police searched for Jack Whitefeather and the twins, it was Scott Cudmore who successfully found them at Dead Man's Cliff. The fire set by former Detective George Burke also burned the body of Jack Whitefeather, consuming the area where he had taken the children. An investigation is underway to find more answers.

Timothy Banford is a staff reporter for The Oakwood Chronicler and can be reached at OakwoodChronicler@gmail.com

Chapter 28
Burning Confessions
July 26th

Scott sat on the floor of a room in the Daye Psychiatric Wing of the Oakwood Island Hospital. The room was quiet except for the occasional sounds the kids made while playing nearby. He folded up the Oakwood Chronicler he had been reading and glanced at his wife through heavy and tired eyes. Miriam was seated on an orange plastic chair on the opposite side of the room. She sat near Patrick, who played with simple wooden blocks on the coffee table and Lily played with a Barbie doll. Scott knew Miriam worried about him as he hadn't slept well since the day of the abduction. The same day Bradley had been murdered. He had been plagued with nightmares of Jack stabbing the children with a bone, over and over. He would wake screaming in terror every time he tried to sleep.

Lily sat in a green plastic chair in front of Monique Richardson.

"Like my dolly?" Lily asked Monique as she stroked the perfectly coiffed hair of the doll. "Her name is Bessie. She wears lots of pretty clothes. She has a blue dress, a red dress and some blue pants too," Lily continued with a nod and a smile as she stroked the yellow flower print dress the doll was currently wearing.

"She's pretty," Monique replied as she wondered why Lily wasn't tearing this doll apart like she used to. "But why did you call her Bessie?" she asked as she glanced at Scott but watched Lily carefully.

"I don't know. Patrick said I should call her that," Lily replied with a shrug.

"Patrick? Where did you hear that name, Bessie?" Monique inquired.

"Bessie, like the woman who used to come see me at night when Mommy and Daddy were asleep," Patrick replied as he carefully stacked bigger blocks on top of smaller blocks by feeling them one at a time. "But she doesn't come anymore. Not since we went for a drive with Jack."

Scott wiped away a tear as he listened, while Miriam, who was tougher emotionally than Scott, watched her husband more than the kids.

"Patrick, why do you think Bessie doesn't come see you anymore?" Monique asked as her gaze went back and forth between the children.

"I don't know," Patrick replied as he tore down the stacks of blocks he had made. "Jack smelled funny," Patrick added. "He smelled like when we go camping and we make a fire to make s'mores. He smelled before he died, but he doesn't smell like that anymore."

Scott was clearly bothered by this statement. They had found the body right where it had lain when Jack died. Although when they found it, he was badly burned, and crows had pecked at the remains. Scott had insisted on seeing the body, had gone down to the morgue and got into an argument with hospital staff that refused to let him see the body. He had wanted to see the body in hopes that it would stop the dreams. Sadly, seeing the body, or rather what was left of it, hadn't helped him sleep any better.

"Can we go home now?" Lily asked. "Bessie is tired and wants to nap," Lily added as she gently stroked her doll's hair.

"Sure," Monique replied. "But I'd like to come visit you soon. Would you like that?"

Lily nodded and smiled.

"Sure," Patrick said. "If it's ok with Mommy and Daddy."

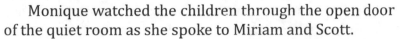

Monique watched the children through the open door of the quiet room as she spoke to Miriam and Scott.

"Children often have strange ways of dealing with trauma," Monique said. "But Lily seems more than fine. I remember when I saw her last time; she was so quiet, hardly ever spoke and never smiled. It's as if all this has done her good, both of them actually. Patrick seems much less anxious now than before. He used to never want to leave his sister's side. Now he doesn't seem to need her as much. I'm thinking maybe he doesn't feel she needs him as much now that she's better. It's too soon to tell, but I'd like to come see them at home. See how they are at home too, if that's ok with you."

"Of course," Scott replied. "That would be great."

"Bradly's death must have been hard on Samantha, even if she's trying not to show it. Being brave for the other kids and all so I'd really like to see Samantha and all the boys. I want to see how they're all doing and how they're dealing with all this."

"I'd like that," Miriam replied as she glanced at Scott, hinting that she would like Monique to speak to him as well.

"Maybe the whole family can see me," Monique replied, picking up on Miriam's subtle clues. "It would do you all good to talk about it," she said while looking directly at Scott.

"That would be great," Scott replied, clearly exhausted. "Thank you."

Just down the hall from where the Cudmores were meeting with their psychiatrist, a patient was tucked away. He had been placed at the end of the long hallway, ironically in the very room where Norah Jenkins had once spent many hours staring in the distance. The patient that had taken over her room was on edge ever since he had been admitted. The nurses had predicted that this patient would be in their care for as long as, if not longer than Norah had.

The air in former Detective Burke's room at the Daye Psychiatric Ward was warm. It seemed cruel to him that he couldn't even remove his own blanket to cool himself, as he was restrained to his bed at the ankles and wrists. He had left them no choice but to restrain him when he had yet another outburst clawing at his own face and neck, scratching himself bloody.

"I burned it, Jin. I burned it all," Burke yelled, his voice echoing in the small room. "I burned it, Jin. I BURNED IT!" Burke shouted until he choked on his dry throat, coughing until he caught his breath. He pulled and tugged at the restraints, trying to move, but failed.

"I told them I did it. I told them I killed them all, Jin. So they wouldn't look for it, Jin."

Burke struggled against his bonds more, making himself even warmer, sweat beading on his forehead, his face turning a bright shade of red.

"I told them it was me. I told them I killed them, Jin. I told them I killed them. So they wouldn't find it and so they won't know our secret. I killed them all and then burned them so our secret stays safe and so nobody knows. I KILLED THEM ALL!"

Burke's voice echoed as a nurse rushed in, syringe in hand, ready to quiet down their most recent arrival.

Chapter 29
The Awakening
July 26ᵗʰ

Shelley served up the day's lunch special; fried bologna, scalloped potatoes and a side of mixed vegetables. She placed the plates before a smiling elderly couple who came for the lunch specials as often as they could.

The restaurant was filled with most of the usual crowd of regulars. Shelley rushed behind the counter, scooped up two readied plates, and left four more paper orders for the day's special to the cook. She brought the plates to Gertrude Dawson who sat by the front windows with her friend Cindy. "Did you hear about Norah?" Gertrude asked as she grabbed Shelley's hand before she could walk away.

"Hear what?" Shelley asked, her curiosity for gossip getting the better of her, more than she would ever admit.

Gertrude looked at Cindy as if to tell her it was her turn to speak, as if to say she should be the one to tell Shelley. Especially since Cindy worked at the hospital, as if it would add validation to the rumors.

"They said when she died...she had water in her lungs," Cindy said, bringing her voice down so not too many people could hear.

"I heard she had pneumonia. That's what killed her," Shelley replied, feeling somewhat miffed that she hadn't heard these rumors until now. "Well, what I heard is that it wasn't just ordinary water," Cindy paused, drawing out the tension, and the attention on her. "It was sea water." She said it in a way that was supposed to amaze Shelley.

"Yeah right!" Shelley replied with a smile. "Sea water... in her lungs. She was on the second floor of the hospital, far away from any sea water." Shelley laughed and walked away, getting back to work. She gathered two more read-ied plates, plopping one on the counter before Doctor Kingsley who was sipping coffee.

"Hey, Doc. That stuff's not good for you," Officer Brent Bartlet said with a smile from the table he shared with officers Paul Malloy and Patricia Clifford. They always took the same table near the counter.

Shelley placed a plate in front of Reverend Masterson who set his copy of The Oakwood Chronicler down and smiled at her. She picked up the empty plate in front of Father Thompson who sat across from the Reverend. The good Father smiled and winked at her as he picked his teeth with a toothpick.

"Delicious as usual," Father Thompson said.

"Thank you," Reverend Masterson said to Shelley as he picked up his fork while Father Thompson took the news-paper from the table.

"Do you mind if I..." he asked but hadn't waited for a reply as he flipped the paper to the front page.

"Help yourself," Reverend Masterson replied as he cut into the fried bologna.

"What a tragedy," Father Thompson muttered as he read that day's front page articles.

"He was here, you know," Shelley said as she stood by the table holding Father Thompson's empty plate.

"Who?" the Reverend asked.

"Detective Burke," Shelley replied, using his title out of habit. "He was here almost every day."

"There was no way to know," Father Thompson interjected. "Evil hides in plain sight and we just don't see it."

"Amen to that," the Reverend added.

"He hated Grady," Shelley added. "I should have seen it, said something. He called him idiot all the time. He was just a kid," Shelley added, wiping away a tear with her shoulder.

"It's probably a good thing you didn't say anything," Father Thompson replied, which got a strange look from Reverend Masterson. "Who knows what would have happened if you did."

"Father Thompson!" Reverend Masterson said in an attempt to scold the good father.

"He might have killed you too," Father Thompson continued.

Shelley walked away, bringing the dirty dishes back behind the counter.

"I heard you had quite the crowd for breakfast this morning," Doctor Kingsley inquired.

"Yeah," Shelley replied. "I had a ton of reporters asking questions."

"Reporters?" Officer Patricia Clifford piped in inquisitively.

"Big newspaper and television reporters looking to do stories on the Disemboweler murders," Shelley said to whomever was listening, which was most everyone. "They also asked a lot about Jack and the twins; about Patrick, the boy born with no eyes."

"A bunch of them were out on Edge this morning," Gertrude added, referring to Ocean's Edge Road. It was obvious she was referring to the reporters.

Shelley grabbed a rectangular plastic tub she used to clear tables with. "They asked a lot of questions about Jack," She added while collecting dishes off the counter.

"He was a quiet man," Doctor Kingsley replied with

sarcasm. "Isn't that what they all say when someone snaps and loses their mind and murders a bunch of people?"

Gertrude leaned in and whispered to her friend Cindy. "Rumor is that Scott owed Jack money for drugs and Jack tried to get Scott to pay him." Gertrude nodded at what she herself had said, as if to confirm it was true.

"Pfft," Cindy replied as she knew better. She worked with Miriam enough to know Scott didn't do drugs. "Scott's a good man, as good as they come. I call bullshit on that."

Shelley busied herself collecting payment from the old couple and clearing the table, collecting the dirty dishes into her plastic tub and wiping down the table. Shelley and the couple exchanged pleasantries as they readied themselves to leave.

"What the hell is that supposed to be?" Cindy uttered in a loud voice.

Many of the patrons turned to look at Cindy, who sat by the large windows in the front of the restaurant. Gertrude and Cindy were both looking outside; their eyes glued to whatever had captured their attention.

"What the hell is what?" Shelley asked as she turned to look in the direction they were staring.

In the middle of the street there strode a barefoot brown skinned woman who wore what Shelley would later assume to be a Halloween costume. A long, ornate-flowing brown robe adorned with beads, hundreds of black feathers, and small things that looked like little sticks or small bones decorated her slim and tall figure. Large gold hooped earrings were combined with little bones, beads, and feathers in her hair as well. The woman carried a gnarled, old wooden walking stick as she strode barefoot down the middle of the street, examining her surroundings with what looked to be utter fascination and curiosity.

"Meh," Doctor Kingsley said, who was looking through

the window at the woman from where he sat at the counter. "You people need to leave this island more often. There's a whole world out there," he added as he went back to sipping the rest of his coffee.

"Cindy!" Shelley said. "I didn't think you, of all people wou..." Shelley stopped in mid-sentence when she saw what Cindy saw.

"That!" Cindy blurted, pointing outside. "What the fuck is that?"

Following the woman down the street were critters and animals the likes of which made this scene even stranger. There were little grey mice, brown filthy rats and cats of various colors and sizes following the woman as if she was the Pied Piper of Hamelin himself. Even stranger still were the snakes that slithered alongside them while crows swooped in, landing on nearby perches of all sorts to watch as she and her animal followers walked past them. Crows took flight and others replaced them swooping in and leaving just as fast. Coming up the rear of the small parade of sorts was one lone wolf who strode with caution, glancing all around at his surroundings.

"What the fuck is that?" Cindy asked again, as people gathered around her to peer outside, a few with phones to record the strangest sight many of them had ever laid eyes on. Thunder rumbled in the distance as the wind picked up, sending small vortexes of dust tumbling up and down the street, in front of the bizarre woman and the animals that followed behind her. Just as she passed the windows of the Old Mill, the skies blackened, and heavy rain poured down from the storm clouds above. The rains would fall heavy, but not as heavy as the worries of the residents of Oakwood Island soon to come.

THE END

Author's Note

Assuming you're reading this book after having read *Oakwood Island*, then by now you know how this book began, with three short stories written by Angella Cormier. Eventually, we started collaborating to expand those three short stories into *Oakwood Island*.

We like to think about those three little short stories like crisp white snowballs rolling down the side of a generous slope. The next thing we knew, those little snowballs were gathering speed and growing in size. Soon we knew we simply had to return to the mystical island as things were brewing, still. Although those snowballs had grown exponentially, there was still a long way to get to the bottom of this imaginary hill. And even now, as you finished reading this second volume, those snowballs are still rolling, gathering speed and growing in size.

What does that mean? It means, dear reader, that we will get back to you soon with a third volume in the Oakwood Island series.

About the Authors

Angella Cormier grew up in Saint Antoine, a small town in south east New Brunswick, Canada. This is where her love of reading and writing was born. Her curious nature about everything mysterious and paranormal helped carve the inspiration for her current passion of writing horror and mystery stories. She is also a published poet, balancing out her writing to express herself in these two very opposing genres. Angella is a mother of two boys as well as an established freelancer in graphic design. Previous titles include *Dark Tales for Dark Nights* published in 2013 (written under Angella Jacob), *Oakwood Island*, and *A Maiden's Perspective: A collection of thoughts, reflections and poetry* published in 2015. For more information, please visit: www.MysteriousInk.ca

Pierre C Arseneault, is the youngest of eleven children and grew up in the small town of Rogersville, New Brunswick, Canada. He fulfilled a childhood goal in 2004 and became a published cartoonist. His first published work of fiction was in 2013; a collection of short stories called *Dark Tales for Dark Nights*; written in collaboration with Angella Cormier. This was followed up by *Sleepless Nights*, a collection of short stories published in 2014, and *Oakwood Island*. His first non-horror novel, *Poplar Falls: The Death of Charlie Baker* was published in 2019. Pierre currently lives in Moncton, New Brunswick, Canada.